DEAD BOY WALKING

I0551786

Rod Martinez

DEAD BOY WALKING

DOUBLE DRAGON

A DOUBLE DRAGON PAPERBACK

© Copyright 2022
Rod Martinez

The right of Rod Martinez to be identified as author of
this work has been asserted in accordance with the
Copyright, Designs and Patents Act 1988

All Rights Reserved

No reproduction, copy or transmission of the publication
may be made without written permission. No paragraph
of this publication may be reproduced, copied or
transmitted save with the written permission of the
publisher, or in accordance with the provisions of the
Copyright Act 1956 (as amended).

Any person who does any unauthorised act in relation to
this publication may be liable to criminal prosecution
and civil claims for damages.

ISBN 978-1-78695-821-1

Double Dragon
is an imprint of
Fiction4All

This Edition Published 2022
Fiction4All
www.fiction4all.com

Cover art by Jenna Genio

DEDICATION

This story is dedicated to my son,
a huge Michael Jackson and *Back To The Future* fan
(You'll get that as you read on…)

PROLOGUE

Brian stood by himself on the wet grass. Though he was surrounded by many of his friends he felt totally alone. It was a semi-gloomy day – weather-wise and emotionally - for him and many other people, and the circumstances of him standing here only made it worse. Brian E. Hill was somewhat of a loner, though the teenager had many friends in school, this was one day he felt like he was the only person on the planet.

"Ashes to ashes, dust to dust… he is in a better place. He was a good friend, a son, a brother, a grandson, and a cousin. His laughter touched many, his smile soothed many, his pranks may have angered many… but Erik Jason Quince will rest in peace - for now, for all of eternity."

The minister closed his Bible in a hushed tone after he uttered the statement and glanced around at the people gathered. Most were teenagers, obviously friends of Erik from school, but many were grownups, maybe family or family of family. The minister rested sight on Brian, who seemed most hit by the loss – aside from the parents.

Brian had a full face and short dark hair that was curly on top. Usually, he sported a jovial face but today he was so serious. He turned around, his classmate Jordan was standing right behind him and both of them had tears in their eyes. There was more reason for their grief than just being at a funeral, these two friends had a history with their dead friend – and this history would haunt them for days or years to come. The way he died would forever be etched on their brains, you see - Erik was their best friend. Brian turned and motioned for Jordan to join him and they both approached their dead friend's parents, Erik's mother was overcome in tears, and her husband held her close, wiping tears from his eyes as well.

"Mrs. Quince," Brian tried to face her, but he stared down instead, "…I'm so sorry…"

"*Don't speak to me!*" she screamed.

Everyone there at the funeral was witness to that outburst. Her broken voice was so loud that some people jumped when she belted out those four words in anger, she couldn't hide her Hispanic accent, and she couldn't hide her rage either. The words spewed from her lips like swords of wrath. Jordan took Brian by the arm and cautiously pulled him away.

"C'mon, Brian. I think we need to go."

The two high school students and Erik were known as *the Quatro* by many at school, *quatro* – meaning *four* in Spanish – they were in Spanish class and AP American History class together as well as marching and concert bands. The remaining member of the group, Elizabeth, was standing further off under an umbrella with her mother. She didn't say a word the whole service, of everyone there, she felt most to blame.

"Family and friends, the Quince family would like to thank you all for being here on this rainy day, to share in their time of grief and sorrow. The original plans were to meet at the Quince home after the funeral, but they uh..." the minister turned to Erik's father, he shook his head 'no', "... instead, they request you give a donation in Erik's name to the charity of your choice. This will conclude the funeral services for Erik J. Quince. May the Lord bless you all."

It was a Saturday, a day none of the friends would ever forget, after all, it was only a week ago, and an incident ago that something happened that caused them all to be out here, standing in the rain at a Brandon, Florida cemetery.

"A week ago today," Elizabeth muttered, the three friends were sitting together at Mariposa's Bakery – a popular eatery in the small Florida community of Brandon, which was just east of the Tampa Bay area, "... I can't believe it, guys. We were in here a week ago and..."

She burst into tears. Brian reached over and held her in a reassuring embrace, but his eyes were teary too. Elizabeth, a senior at Victoria High in Brandon, was considered the leader of their little group, she was the cornerstone, 'the rock' as Erik used to call her. Jordan looked away. Right after the funeral, the three decided to meet at their favorite hang-out instead of at Davis Park where many of the other friends from school decided to attend a bar-b-que fundraiser in Erik's name.

Jordan saw the look of despair on Elizabeth's face. Normally she was always the one in the chipper mood, smiling and getting everyone else on task.

"Elizabeth, we need to pull ourselves together, Erik wouldn't want this, you know, us mourning over him like this," Jordan said.

Brian turned to him, in disbelief and forced a smile.

"Are you kidding? Erik *always* wanted to be the center of attention; he'd be gloating through all this in that silly smile of his."

The three friends stared around at each other as smiles slowly crept onto their young faces.

"Ha, you know he's right." she sniffed.

Jordan was shaking his head in a smile as he felt someone brush up next to him.

"Guys, sorry to hear about Erik, he and I knew each other since fourth grade. I know you guys were really close. I'm going to miss him, you know?" Morgan said, walking up to them, "… why didn't you guys go to the bar-b-que?"

"Because we're *the Quatro* and Erik was a member of *the Quatro*, so everyone would be on us, you know, asking about that day… and we, we…"

"We don't feel like answering questions anymore," Jordan said finishing Brian's statement.

"Well don't worry – I won't ask you guys any questions. I know this has been hard on all of us who were really close to him." Morgan reassured.

She was also a friend but didn't hang with this group so much, Morgan was an Honor Roll student that was in the band with all four friends, but she was in a different circle, yet she knew Erik more than any other friend at Victoria High.

"Yeah, this isn't going to be easy on any of us, especially with his family blaming us for it."

Morgan looked down at the group leader who was still wiping her tears.

"We'll get through this Elizabeth; Erik meant a lot to a lot of people." Morgan smiled.

"Yeah," Brian shrugged," … but it isn't fair. Why'd he have to die?"

The three friends got up and walked toward the door.

CHAPTER 1

Brian Hill's first day at Victoria High back in his freshman year was awkward. He wanted to join the band but didn't really know how to play any instrument, he sat in on the orientation and the band teacher picked the tuba for him. Usually, the bigger kids get picked the bigger instruments and Brian fit that equation, not that he had an issue with it, but he asked for percussion. He was later told that he'd be accommodated. He didn't mind, Brian was a very easy-going type and quickly got along with everyone. He was like everybody's little or big brother, depending on what age you were or what grade you were in. He was the last joining member to make *the Quatro… the Quatro*.

Elizabeth Baker was handed a clarinet, Jordan a trumpet. Erik played sax. He was already a sax player, he'd been playing since fifth grade and he was good. They all got to know each other that year, the band turned out to be more like a family instead of just another class, and the friends quickly bonded; each of them had come from a different middle school.

Jordan Lunas and his parents lived in an affluent neighborhood of Brandon, he could easily have had his pick of friends, but he blended in nicely with *the Quatro* when the four first met on the very first day of band camp. Jordan and Erik were bunkmates. Brian slept on the bunk next to them with Peter – who was in percussion.

Morgan and Elizabeth were bunkmates on the girl's side of band camp. Morgan, a blonde who didn't really fuss with her hair and liked to wear Adventure Time hats, looked like she was into athletics – but she wasn't.

She and Erik's families were friends, so they saw a lot of each other and even went on vacations together. Morgan was a free spirit, and she didn't socialize much.

Elizabeth Baker was a tall brunette who looked like she belonged on the cover of a fashion magazine, but she didn't act like it. Her first meeting with Erik was during the summer just before first-year band camp for them. The school had a team spirit event at the Campbell's Ice Cream shop on Parsons.

Erik and Elizabeth had both separately ordered the exact same sundae, and when the girl brought it out, they both grabbed it and sent ice cream back into the server's face.

"That was my ice cream!" Erik yelled.

"I beg to differ, it was mine. But you can have it now." She smiled.

"Man, that sucks." He said.

"No, you suck." She pointed.

The band teacher walked up to the two.

"Ok children, you both are going to be a part of my band, and there's a rule in the band. We don't fight, we're family. I suggest both of you buy each other another one and get over it."

She walked away.

"Did she just call us children?" Erik smirked.

Elizabeth laughed while wiping whipped cream off her forehead.

"Yep, I believe she did, but she's right. So what do you want? My treat."

Erik shone his famous smile, they became friends that day.

Morgan was also at the ice cream social, but she didn't socialize with many. The new freshman quickly was set apart from a lot of her friends. While in band camp, which was across the state in some remote forest region close to Ocala, the blonde sat alone a lot and stared out into the woods. There were times she'd sit there and not communicate with any of her friends; something had her glued to the spooky woods just outside of their camp. On a couple of nights, the camp director would tell scary stories about ghosts of the region and their relationships to this camp.

"During the Civil War, Captain Armwood Harrington – an officer of the Confederate Army - and his regiment massacred a platoon of Union forces right here on this land. It was a bloody battle and Union Captain Elijah Oliver and his men lost their lives. They were beheaded at the lake... and their blood sank deep into the soil. Some say their headless corpses come out late at night in the mist from the lake here looking for other heads to replace theirs. The soldiers were young, some as young as you are. Make sure you lock your cabins tonight…"

The kids would scare easily, except for Morgan who'd stare at the camp director then glare out into the woods with an eerie smirk. Erik was the only one she'd let into her world, and whatever was going on, they kept it secret.

That first day of High School was uncomfortable for Brian, an outgoing friendly type who had learned more than once that not everyone else was as outgoing as he was, or as friendly. On the first day, Erik approached him when he saw Brian lend lunch money to another student, then the student kept coming back, every day.

"Ok Johnny, this is going to stop. You can't keep taking money off Brian, you get lunch, what are you, saving up for college? Don't jocks have scholarships for that?"

"Keep outta this Quince!" the tall student said.

"Or what? You going to bench press me?"

Johnny was six feet two inches tall and on the football and wrestling teams, Erik was five seven and thin as a rail, but Erik learned back in elementary school not to back down to bullies, he was used to this. He'd gotten written up in fifth grade for punching the school bully in the face. That didn't sit right with him, Jacob was the bully – but Erik got in trouble.

"Punk, you challenging me?" Johnny huffed.

"Na, see challenge wouldn't exactly be quite the right word, Frankenstein. And I call you Frankenstein in reverence – after all that is what you are, right? A big lug made of by-products? Anyway, Neanderthal, my buddy Brian here ain't giving you a red cent from now on, that's all there is to it."

"Neanderthal? Are you insulting me, dweeb?"

"See? It's so easy even a caveman can understand." He smiled patting Brian on the shoulder.

No one in school ever challenged Johnny Bernard Goode and lived to tell about it, much less spoke down to him the way Erik did. Johnny reached out to grab Erik and found himself instead in the air, when Erik grabbed his fist, bent over, and threw him over his side – the muscular jock then landed on the principal's prize rose bush. Just in time for the principal to walk out and catch him screaming in pain from the thorns as he tried to get out. Mrs. Diriscall was not in a happy mood after that with Johnny. Erik and Brian had already walked away.

"Man dude, Johnny's probably going to get both of us for that." Brian smiled nervously.

"I can handle his type, hey after school a bunch of us in band are going to the Brandon Music Showcase store to check out some musical equipment, I need more reeds for my new sax. Then we're going to Mariposa's, you coming?"

"What's a Mariposa's?"

"Brian, Brian," Erik smiled, "… dude, you need to get out more. It's a bakery about a half mile from here. You in? You can ask your Mom to pick you up there instead of here at school, or one of the guys can take you home. We were going to talk about some band stuff, then pig out on Cuban sandwiches."

Erik always had this confident smile that shone on his dark skin. A dark-skinned Hispanic was something new to Brian, but he soon came to learn that it was something common in the Tampa Bay area.

"Sure Erik, sounds like fun. I love Cuban sandwiches."

They became best friends that day.

CHAPTER 2

Elizabeth walked out of the bathroom at home in her PJs and went to the kitchen where her mom was baking a cake. She sat at the table in a solemn mood, she was still in mourning.

"Elizabeth honey, are you ok?"

"No Mom... I don't know how any of us will ever be the same again."

Her mother put the large spoon down; she was putting the icing on the cake. The look on her daughter's face wasn't a look she was used to; she put her arm around Elizabeth's shoulder.

"Honey, this is going to be a trying time for all of us. Remember the first time I met him, that Halloween? I didn't know what he was supposed to be and I asked 'The Walking Dead? No ma'am, a zombie from the Michael Jackson Thriller video' and then he started doing the moves. I fell in love with that boy that day. Erik was close to a lot of people."

"I know Mom... but his parents, you know, they won't even talk to us now."

"Elizabeth, I would do the same thing if I were in their shoes. Erik was their only son."

"Gee, thanks, Mom."

"I'm just saying, Honey. You have to understand – from the viewpoint of a parent... a part of their soul was taken away from them."

Elizabeth started crying and ran off to her room.

At Brian's house, he was sitting in his room, staring at the television – which wasn't even on. His mother walked in with the bowl of garbanzo bean soup he had asked for. He was so distraught and she didn't quite know what to do.

"Here you go, Honey."

She placed it on the nightstand, but he didn't budge.

"Sorry Mom, I keep turning around, thinking, you know - he's going to hop in that door doing the moonwalk, or showing me the new watch, he just got or… I don't know, burping loud as he does. You know, I never did understand his fascination with watches."

She sat on the bed, rubbed his back in a caring swipe, and turned and looked into his watery eyes.

"He's gone, Mom. Erik's really gone."

"I know Honey. I was talking to Elizabeth's mom and poor Elizabeth is so distraught. She's helping her mother bake a cake. She wanted you and the gang to deliver it to Erik's family."

"Are you kidding me? They hate us! Erik's parents despise *the Quatro*."

"They don't hate you, Brian, true they may blame you all for… well, you know, but…"

"Mom, how was it our fault!?" he started crying and she held him.

No parent wants to see their child hurting, and Brian was definitely feeling the pain of loss with his friend's death.

Jordan Lunas was sitting on his back porch with his parents and little sister, staring at the pool. The moonlight bounced off the calm water, it was quiet and all they could hear were the crickets.

Jordan wasn't very talkative but his parents understood.

"Jordan, are you sad because of Erik?"

"Yes, Sissy."

"Did you really see him die?"

Sissy was only five years old and the closest she ever got to the subject was when her fish Jack died. She cried, they had a funeral, she put him on a paper boat that Jordan had made and they watched the boat float down the creek in their backyard. Minutes later she was asking for a hamster.

Jordan turned to his father as they sat glaring at the pool.

"Dad? Is there life after death?"

"Son that's a topic that has been debated since the dawn of man, I can't truthfully answer that question… since I haven't kicked the bucket yet." He offered with a smile.

"But it's not fair, he's gone too soon. Erik, he looked so… peaceful in that casket, like you know, like he was sleeping like he was dreaming or something."

"Death is a most peaceful slumber." His mother sighed.

"But he's only seventeen, it's not fair."

"Death doesn't care how old you are, son." His father said.

Jordan looked down at the water in the pool and sighed to himself.

"He looked so peaceful, yeah... it's like he was asleep."

Later that night, Elizabeth was lying in bed; she was staring blankly at the dark ceiling. She knew she'd end up crying herself to sleep and that it would probably be how she fell asleep for the next few weeks. Yet within minutes, she fell fast asleep. It didn't last long, she felt someone shaking her. It couldn't be time to wake up, she'd felt like she'd just fallen asleep.

"Wake up." said the whispered voice.

"Mmmm?"

"Come on... get up?"

Elizabeth slowly sat up and cleared her eyes.

"What, who is it?"

It took seconds for her eyes to focus; the dark eyes staring back at her gave her a chill.

"Erik?"

He smiled.

Their eyes were caught in a glare that lasted longer, about ten seconds then she jumped up on the bed and sat fully.

"No!" she shook her head, "… you're not here!"

Suddenly she jumped violently from her dream and sat up on the bed.

"Erik?"

The tears started to flow.

"Erik, I'm so sorry. I'm never going to get over this. I was there; I should have done something, I…"

CLICK!

It was small, like the sound of a pencil falling off from the dresser to the tiled floor in her room. But the sound came from her closet. She looked over at the closet door, something had moved inside.

"Hello? Fluffy are you in my closet again?"

Elizabeth got up; it wouldn't be the first time her cat decided to roam around in her closet, Fluffy was a very curious yet independent pet. She walked over to the sliding door of her walk-in closet.

"Fluffy, please don't scratch up my scarves again!"

Through the slits of the closet door she saw a shimmering light, it seemed to pulsate on some weird rhythm but it was very small. She slid open the door, prepared for her cat to run out through her legs, but the figure crouched there was not her cat, it wasn't of animal origin at all... it was the figure of a young man, and he slowly stood to his feet. She jumped back, startled for a second then backed off and prepared a scream.

"Lizzy, chill, it's me."

Lizzy, only one person had ever called her by that name. She only *allowed* one person to call her by that name, and that one person wasn't around anymore. That one person was dead, that one person was...

"Erik?" she backed up to her bed where she kept a walking stick that Erik had given to her as a souvenir from his family's Georgia mountains trip last year. She grasped it in her right hand.

"I'm warning you, whoever you are, I have a weapon and I know how to use it! Now step out or there's going to be a hurtin' in here. You can't be Erik, who are you?" she frowned.

He stepped out into the light. The shimmering orange light she saw was from a stone on the ring on his index finger. She'd never seen anything like it before.

"Come on Lizzy, is that any way to greet your best friend?"

She heard the voice, it sounded right, but the ring? That was a new thing. And still, Erik? Alive? In her closet? She froze and squinted her eyes to make sure. She had just woken up from a dream, maybe she was still in the dream.

"Erik?" she cocked her head.

The light from her stereo on the bed crept up his chest and he got closer and ultimately rested on his face where she could finally see for sure.

"Lizzy." he smiled.

She fell back on the bed in a faint.

CHAPTER 3

It was Sunday morning and Brian woke up dead tired. He was restless from the night before and was tossing and turning since the break of dawn. Still wearing the clothes that he wore the day before, he turned and looked at the clock on his nightstand, it was ten o'clock. Where did the time go? He went to bed thinking about Erik, woke up at 2 AM remembering the day it happened, and then again at four breaking a sweat. He thought about Elizabeth and wondered how she was doing. She and he were closest to Erik, hopefully, she was still asleep. He thought to call her and reached for his cell phone and it rang just before he touched it, that startled him for a second then he saw the name.

"Elizabeth."

He sat up on the bed.

"Hey Elizabeth, man I was just thinking about you, was going to call..."

"I saw him, I saw him last night, Brian! He was in my room! I, I can't believe this!" she interrupted.

She was hysterical.

"What? You saw who? Elizabeth calm down, man."

"*Erik,* Brian! I saw Erik last night!"

Silence.

"Brian!?"

"Uh... yeah..?"

25

"Did you hear me!?"

"Uh yeah, I think you said you saw…"

Just then his bedroom door opened and his mom walked in with Jordan right behind her.

"Uh... hold on a sec Elizabeth."

"Honey, Jordan came over. I didn't want to keep him waiting downstairs. I'm making breakfast, would you like to stay for breakfast Jordan?"

"No… no ma'am. Thanks."

"Ok."

She turned and walked out, then turned to her son.

"Uh, Brian Honey, please pick up your room."

"Yes, Mom."

She walked out and closed the door. Brian hit the speaker button on his phone.

"Elizabeth, Jordan is here," he whispered.

"You don't believe me, do you?" she asked in a huff on the speaker, she had been talking the whole time.

"OK, wait, wait, Now tell Jordan what you just told me."

"I saw Erik last night, he was in my closet."

The two friends turned to each other, and both of their eyebrows went up.

"You're both staring at each other, aren't you?"

"You saw Erik?"

"Yes. Then I fainted."

Silence.

"Guys!?"

"Uh, Elizabeth... I don't know how to tell you this, but..."

"Jordan, I'm dead serious, you have to believe me! Have I ever lied to you?"

"No, you haven't Elizabeth, but see uh... you say you saw Erik last night, well the thing is, I think I did too." Jordan sighed.

"Whew... so did I," Brian confessed.

"Well, we all know that's not possible, what's going on?" Jordan asked.

She was brushing her teeth, they could hear it.

"I don't know," she said rinsing her mouth, "... but I'm driving over to the cemetery and find out."

"Well come get us! We wanna go too!"

Elizabeth was the only one of the friends who had a car, a minivan to be exact.

"Brian, pancakes!" his mother called up the stairs.

"Ok, well come get us after breakfast!" he said.

"*Geez-a.*" She sighed.

"His mom makes the best pancakes; I think I'm going to eat too," Jordan said.

"How can you guys think of eating at a time like this!?" she fumed.

"Geez Elizabeth, just get here in like ten minutes, we'll be ready!" Jordan pressed the end key on Brian's iPhone then he turned to his friend.

"You have to admit, this is a little freaky."

"No, this isn't a little freaky, this is *big-time* freaky, Jordan."

"Are you ready to go?"

"Yeah Jordan, I just need my belt, can you get it for me?" he was tying his shoes.

"Where do you keep it?"

"I keep it in the closet."

"Brian!" his mom screamed again.

Jordan grabbed it and they ran down the stairs.

CHAPTER 4

The blue Honda Odyssey quickly cruised down Brandon Boulevard with the three friends inside. It was a solemn moment for all of them, none of them said a single word. Jordan had just *Snap Chatted* his little sister with a picture of the cemetery sign and wrote "*Ooooo spooky*".

Elizabeth knew where she was going, but the two other friends didn't actually pay attention to the road. They rarely drove anyway, though Jordan was now the owner of his Mom's old Mustang, it was sitting in his garage waiting for the family mechanic to repair it.

Brian looked out and pointed at the cemetery sign.

"Hillsboro Memorial Cemetery. My best friend is lying in here," he said.

"*Our* best friend is lying in here!" Elizabeth added.

"Yeah." He looked away.

The van came to a slow halt down the gravel drive. Jordan turned to Brian, who was sitting in the back. Brian seemed most emotionally hit by Erik's death and the two friends tended to overprotect him.

"You going to be ok, bro?" Jordan asked.

Jordan was a thin-framed, skater-looking type, but he didn't own a skateboard. His hair was light brown and moussed up in front though he was constantly sweeping it back in a one-hand gesture. Brian once told Jordan that he reminded him of Shaggy from Scooby Doo, if Shaggy had short hair.

Among the four friends, Jordan was most different from them, but he blended in well. He had a laid-back attitude that had almost rivaled Erik's, except Erik, could get obsessive about things at times. It was Jordan's famous laugh that caught Erik's attention the first time they met. It was almost more of a grunt instead of a laugh, Erik told him he sounded like a motorcycle trying to get started. Jordan Lunas was a self-proclaimed *Back To The Future* expert. He first watched the movie when he was a six-year-old with his dad on DVD and was smitten by the movie, so much so that he had to have the entire trilogy. He knew everything, every detail, every line, every song and that came to a challenge when Erik once misquoted a line and said, "we should put a Flux Capulator in this school bus, then we'd get to school on time."

"Uh, that's Flux *Capacitor*, dude." Jordan corrected.

"Hey, I just watched the movie last night on USA, it's Capulator," Erik argued.

"Trust me, Quince, it's Capacitor."

"Wanna bet?" he challenged the Back To The Future expert.

Jordan sat up on the seat and stared at Erik's G-Shock watch. It was a different-looking kind of watch and Erik wore it all the time, he had a thing for watches, but so did Jordan because of the movie.

"Yeah Q, I betcha your watch that the word is Capacitor."

"What do I get when you lose?"

"*If* I lose, and I won't – I'll take you to the Brandon Mall and buy you a new pair of Converse."

"Dude, you're on, I already know which pair I'll pick!"

Brian pulled out his iPhone and quickly Googled it.

"And the winner is, let's see," he said in a radio announcer voice, "... will Erik J, 'the Q' Quince score a new pair of radical Converse shoes, OR will Jordan 'I know I'm right' Lunas score the coveted G-Shock that never leaves Q's wrist? The tension is on folks..."

He started humming the theme from Jeopardy.

"Come on Brian, stop playing around!" Jordan said.

"Say, say, say... chill out my bruth... ok and it looks like, yes folks, Erik?"

"Yes?" Erik smiled.

"You are wrong; the G-Shock watch goes to its *new* rightful owner, Jordan 'Doc Brown' Lunas. Q, hand it over."

"What? No way man!"

Everybody started laughing, Erik's watch was something everyone knew about, he treated it like a pet. Jordan started laughing and his laugh made everyone else laugh, Erik was pouting.

"I'm just kidding Q, I don't want your watch, bro. But you'll know better than to challenge me in BTTF knowledge, now won't cha, McFly?" Jordan laughed.

That laugh turned Erik's pout into a smile.

Jordan smiled to himself thinking about that day, but then he turned to Brian who was staring out the window with a serious glare. Brian was really close to Erik.

"Hey, Brian – did you hear me?" Jordan asked, his smile quickly faded off.

"Huh?"

"I said are you going to be ok? You don't have to go out there. You can stay in the van, we'd understand."

"Yeah Brian, you can stay…"

"No, I have to do this, guys."

The three stared around at each other.

"Ok."

She parked the van, the three friends walked out and over to the fresh, new tombstone. It was probably the newest on the property. The shade from the tree standing next to it was a relief, the Florida sun was scorching this Sunday morning. Brian stood closest to the grave. Jordan came up behind him. Elizabeth stood back a bit, her eyes started to fill with tears. Brian stepped up and cleared his throat.

"Hi Erik, uh…" he stammered, his bottom lip started shaking, "… uh, we uh… we wanted to come, you know… and see you. I mean, I mean you know, talk to you, and uh…"

He breathed in and lowered his head, he had practiced in his head what he was going to share, but he just didn't know what else to say. Then Jordan walked up from behind Brian.

"Erik, dude. We stopped by to say that we loved you man, and we're sorry, sorry for what happened," he said holding a gulp in his throat, "… it's not fair that you're gone, it's not fair how it happened, it's not fair that – well - we feel to blame in a way, and we just… man we miss you, dude."

He turned to Elizabeth. She was staring at the gravestone.

"You always said that I was the cornerstone of *the Quatro*, but Erik – you know, in reality – you were. We can't be *the Quatro* without you." She sighed.

The three stared around at each other. They stood in total silence as a light warm breeze whisked by them. It was totally peaceful where they stood. The only sound made was of the traffic just yards away whisking down Brandon Boulevard, then…

"Wow guys, I'm moved. I hope you mean that."

They knew the voice, Elizabeth jumped startled and looked up to where the voice came from. There was a shadow in the tree just above them, and then it dropped to the soft ground. He landed on his feet, crouched down, then slowly stood up. Brian's jaw dropped. Jordan's eyebrows curled in disbelief.

"Erik?"

"Ohh…"

Elizabeth fell into a faint and Brian caught her before she hit the ground.

She opened her eyes; she was lying back in her van, in the passenger's seat. Brian was fanning her although the air conditioner was on full blast.

"Elizabeth?" he asked.

She squinted and then focused on him.

"Brian… uh, are we…?"

"We're in your van."

She hopped up and looked outside, they were still at the cemetery.

"Where's Jordan?"

Brian moved and Jordan was sitting in the driver's seat smiling at her.

"Whew, ok… ok I was like, dreaming or something, right? I didn't see what I thought I saw, right? I mean - ha, what with the hot Florida sun, the stress we've all been through, the grief, the, the …"

She looked at Brian, then at Jordan, waiting for them to confirm her statements, but instead, they were both looking behind her. She sat up on the seat and slowly turned around.

"Lizzy, please don't faint again, I'm starting to get a complex up in here."

"Erik! No, *Nooo* you're not here. He's not here, you're not here, right?"

"Elizabeth, Erik is here. He's sitting in your van and he picked you up out there and brought you to the van."

She stared at him, he hadn't really changed at all, he looked the same, same chocolate skin, the same smile, the same curly dark brown hair, same dimples on his cheeks. She took a breath, then looked over at her two friends, then back at him. The weird glow from the ring was pulsating brighter.

"Erik... ok, let me get this straight," she said, "...you really died, right?"

"Uh, yeah."

"Ok and so, I'm not dreaming right?"

"Uh, no."

"Ok is Brian dreaming? Is Jordan dreaming?"

"Uh, no."

"Ok, so... uh, help me understand this because I'm about to lose it here. You died, we were at your funeral, that's your grave over there, but you're sitting in my van with us."

"Yep, that's pretty much it." he smiled.

"O-M-G you're a zombie!" Brian screamed, "... I gotta Snap-Chat this to Morgan!"

"I'm not a zombie, dude. And put the iPhone down."

"Are you sure you aren't a zombie?" Jordan asked.

"I think I'm sure."

"You don't have a yearning to eat our flesh or anything? Maybe bite Brian's arm off?"

"Dude, that's gross." Erik chuckled.

They stared around at each other, all four of them. The silence was unnerving.

"Ok I'll ask," Elizabeth piped up, "… I'll just ask, because see, all three of us are asking this in our heads, right? Right? Erik… *how is this possible*!?"

The three friends stared at him. He leaned back on the seat and looked outside for a few seconds.

"You know guys, that funeral was really something, I mean seeing how all you guys felt about me, man even Mrs. Diriscall was crying. I made a principal cry. That was awesome."

"Erik."

"No really, even Morgan's mom who's known me since I was like nine, she was boohooing like a baby. That was really moving."

"Stop changing the subject dude!" Jordan snapped.

"Na man let me bask in this a little, I mean did you see Annie from our Spanish class? The girl treats me like she hates my guts."

"She should, she had a crush on you and you ended up dating her sister!" Elizabeth said.

"Yeah, but did you see her? She was bawling like a baby and her little brother kept asking her, 'Annie are you ok, are you ok Annie?', it was priceless. He stopped and stared at them in a huge smile. They'd lost their patience. All three had their arms folded and were not amused at all. His smile slowly faded off under their frowns.

"Well?" Elizabeth pushed.

He rolled his eyes and sighed.

"To answer your question, it's possible because, well because I made it possible, I guess."

"That doesn't answer the question, dude. How are you not dead?" Jordan asked.

"Well, remember that night? The night that it… happened?"

"Trust me, we will never forget that night, Q." Brian sighed.

Q was his nickname in school among his friends. Most weren't sure if it was because of *the Quatro*, or because of his last name.

"That night is the night that will we be burned forever in our brains." Elizabeth told him.

It all flashed back in their minds. Last Saturday after a band car wash, several members of the Victoria High marching band agreed to meet at Mariposa's for Cuban sandwiches. Erik's mother texted him to come straight home because they had to get him fitted for a tux for his sister's wedding. He replied back.

"At Mariposa's will be home in thirty."

Then they walked into the establishment, but he pulled out his wallet and realized that he didn't have cash, he wanted cash because he owed Elizabeth ten bucks for gas money.

"Be right back guys, going across the street to the ATM. If I don't give Lizzy her ten bucks, I'll be walking home."

"Q, you can give me the money in school on Monday."

"Na, my Dad always says pay your debts."

"Geez, well hurry man I'm starved!" Jordan said.

Erik ran across the street to the bank out there on the corner. The friends started looking at all the goodies on display in the bakery. Brian walked up to the counter to make his order; the place was packed as usual. Elizabeth walked over to the pastries section.

"Mm meat pies, they're the bomb here!"

Jordan was looking at the sandwiches. Brian had already made his order when he heard the police sirens outside.

"Man, what's going on out there and why is Erik taking so long?"

Then they heard the scream. It came from inside the bakery, from a girl standing next to the window. They turned, it was Sasha, a fellow classmate from school, she was looking out in horror and started pointing in the direction across the street. Jordan ran to the window and looked out. Someone was lying in the parking lot and people were huddled around him, cops swerved on the scene and some of them burned off down Oakfield Drive heading toward the Publix Supermarket.

"What the...?"

Brian bolted out the door and Elizabeth was close behind.

"Where's Erik!? Where's Q!?" he screamed.

They got there without hesitation and broke through the crowd to witness their worst nightmare. Erik was lying on the pavement, the look on his face, pain, shock – it was unbearable to his friends. They knew... he was dying. He was being held up by a passerby on the street and he was coughing blood all over the place.

"Erik!? Oh my God!" Elizabeth screamed.

"What happened!? *What happened?*" Brian screamed out to those standing nearby.

Jordan broke through and reached them.

"Hey what's goin' on... oh... oh no!"

"Two guys were robbing the bank," one of the witnesses started, "... they ran outside, and this kid here tried to stop them, and... they..."

Erik looked up at his friends, he was slipping fast, his eye rolled up in slow pain.

"Lizzy..." he whispered.

Brian stood up.

"Has anyone called 911!? For Pete's sake!" he pulled out his phone but he was so upset his fingers just kept hitting the 1 after he dialed 9... he just kept hitting the dial pad.

"Erik!? Oh God, oh God, oh God, *noooooo*!" Elizabeth took him in her arms.

"It's ok Lizzy... I'm, gonna be ok... I'm... wow, look at that light..." he smiled, "...tell Mom I love her..." he panted in a last breath.

She looked into his eyes... and his stare turned from a soft smile to stone cold and lifeless in a matter of seconds.

"Erik!? *ERIK!?*" she screamed.

Brian fell to his knees and tried to lift him.

"No! Leave him! Leave him alone!" Elizabeth cried.

She held him close and began trembling in tears.

"Where are the guys that did this!? Where *ARE THEY*!" Jordan screamed.

Several of the witnesses pointed west, where Publix was. Jordan hopped up and ran off in that direction, why? He had no idea, but he felt like he had to do something.

The scene was fresh on all of their minds as they sat in the van and listened to Erik re-tell it. And all of them had tears in their eyes.

"And uh... they took me to the hospital. I heard them pronounce me dead. I heard Mom and Dad come in and mom lost it. You ever heard an angry Cuban woman crying and cursing at the top of her lungs?"

"Uh actually, yeah Erik, we have... your Mom hates us now."

"It wasn't your fault."

"Yeah, we know that, but your mom thinks it was, and I think your sister wants to kill us."

"Erik... uh, how does it feel? I mean, you're d... you're d... you're not alive anymore, and..."

She reached out to touch him, he was cold to the touch, and she yanked her hand back.

"Uh, I don't quite get what's going on myself, Lizzy."

"So, wait a minute," Brian said, "... so, you got killed by bank robbers, they took you away to the hospital, you died, we were at your funeral, and you're sitting here in Elizabeth's car. And you don't even know what happened? Or how it happened?"

Brian scratched his head.

"See? Oh snap you *are* a zombie!" he screamed pointing at him.

"Brian, I'm *not* a zombie!"

"Yes you are, yes you are! You're going to want to eat our flesh, and suck our brains out, and make blood soup, and..."

"Brian!" he reached out and took hold of his friend's arm.

"I am *not* a zombie man! And to be honest, I don't even feel hunger. I feel like I'm in a daze, you know? It's like I'm here and not here at the same time. You know how you feel when you have a cold, and your mom gives you

Nyquil? That's how I feel right now, this is just… weird."

"Q, I don't understand," Jordan said, "… ok you died, you're here... what gives? Not that we don't want you back here. We're *the Quatro* again, this is tight, but, but… I don't get it."

"I don't either, dude."

"Maybe… maybe you were spared so you can clear your murder?"

"Really, Elizabeth?"

"Brian, for your information, I've read about stories like that."

"Well, this isn't one of your fiction stories from your Kindle, Elizabeth, this is real life!"

The four friends glared around each other in the van.

"Well, I don't know what to do. I mean, I know I can't go home, Mom would probably wig out. I can't hang with you guys because everyone knows I'm dead. I've got no place to go."

"Dude you can stay in the pool house in my back yard." Jordan smiled.

"Yeah, but I can't just stay here… not that I don't want to be here – but, I know there's a reason I'm here. I saw the light; you know that light people always talk about when they have those near-death experiences? It's real, I saw it, I felt it. It's like a freaking magnet, like when I'm in the mall and I pass the watch store, I *have* to go in. So, there I was, but I just didn't feel compelled to go."

"How did it feel?" Brian asked.

"Well, there was uh, like a tunnel and the light came from the end but it was overpowering and covered everything. And it was like something inside you is compelled to go to it. You can't fight it."

"But you did."

"Yeah Jordan, but I wasn't alone in there... someone else was in the white room with me and he pointed back and I looked back and there I was lying there, and I saw the nurse turn to the doctor and say, 'He's dead, Jim.'... and I kinda floated out the door. You know how they say you see your whole life flash in front of you? I did, and it was in the blink of an eye."

"That's creepy, dude." Brian said.

"You can say that again."

"That's creepy dude."

Erik rolled his eyes.

"Who was the person in there with you, what did he look like?"

"I didn't really see him Lizzy, I felt him. It's hard to explain."

Elizabeth looked into his eyes; his pupils were jet black. They used to be brown.

Erik curled down on the seat, his hand quickly covered his chest and the ring on his finger started glowing bright.

"Erik?"

"I don't feel so good." he said.

"You don't look so good." Brian replied.

43

"I need to… I need to go." He told them, it almost looked like he was holding back some kind of pain, or something.

"Erik?"

He reached for the door latch and pulled the door open.

"Q?"

The look on his face changed, and the light on the ring got even brighter. His face looked like he was going into a trance. Jordan reached out to him, but Erik stepped out of the van, and started walking out into the cemetery.

"Erik!?" Elizabeth called out.

He was outside, walking aimlessly in no particular direction. Jordan was going to hop out of the van and run to him. Elizabeth grabbed his arm.

"Jordan, no… let's see where he goes. We can follow him. It almost looks like something is calling him, whatever it is, we'll follow him."

"What if someone out there sees him? His picture is all over TV and the paper, they'll know who he is."

"Yeah…"

Brian looked out again, Erik suddenly had stopped in his tracks, then turned around to the van. He shook his head, as if in confusion, like he'd just woken up from a dream - then blinked his eyes a couple of times.

"Erik?"

"Brian… what happened?"

"You were like in a trance, man."

He walked back to the van.

"Come on; let's get you to Jordan's pool house!"

Brian yanked his friend back into the van.

"Let's go, Elizabeth."

The van backed out and drove off.

CHAPTER 5

Morgan Rubens was in her backyard with her mother spreading mulch around the trees. The Rubens residence landscape was the envy of many neighborhoods in Brandon. Her mother, an accountant by day – spent a lot of her spare time working in the garden and the yard. Morgan had just dug her hand into the bag of mulch when the phone rang.

"Geez!"

She yanked off her glove and pulled her phone out of her pocket.

"Hello?"

"Morgan, it's Brian."

"Brian? From band? Hey Brian… what...?"

"Morgan, we need you to come to Jordan's house." He interrupted.

"We who?"

"We *the Quatro*. It's important, ok?"

"Now?"

"Yes now!"

"Uh… ok."

The gang had just parked at Jordan's massive home in the driveway. As soon as she turned off the van, the front door to the house opened.

"Oh, snap guys, here comes my dad. Q you need to hide."

46

"Where!?"

"Hop over the back seat!"

"Really?"

"*JUST DO IT*!" all three screamed.

He hopped over the seat and landed on the car jack.

"Ow!"

"Hey Champ, what's going on? What brings the gang over?"

"Uh nothing dad, we were all just going to hang out over at the pool in the back. Are you and Mom going somewhere?" Jordan was hoping he'd say yes.

"No, I'm going over to the Country Club, there's a golf tournament today. Yeah buddy! So, you guys don't mess up the pool, we just got it cleaned, ya know."

"Yes sir." Brian nervously smiled. He kept looking at the back to make sure Erik wouldn't pop his head up.

"You know son," Jordan's father said, "... one of my golf partners today is the Sheriff and he said he was going to start up a trust fund in Erik's name."

"Uh... r-really?"

"Yeah, the two men who robbed that bank are still at large and there's a massive manhunt out for them, with a huge reward. The community has come out in droves. Seems Erik's death has touched a nerve, we don't have stuff like that happen in Brandon. I'm telling you, I feel sorry for those two jerks, when they get caught, they're really gonna pay for it."

"Wow dad, that's great."

"That's moving, Mr. Lunas," Elizabeth said, "…I sure hope they catch them."

"I do too, Elizabeth." he smiled, "… ok, you guys have fun. Your mom's home Jordan, she's out back watering her flowers, I think the gardener is on his way. By the way son, can you come over and move the Mustang, I need to get my Beamer out."

"M-move the Mustang?"

"Yeah, just take it out of the garage, the mechanic was just working on it and we left it there. He left about thirty minutes ago."

Jordan turned to Elizabeth they both looked in the rear-view mirror.

"Ok, Dad. Sure." He widened his eyes at Brian to make sure he'd keep Erik hidden.

Brian nodded. "Have a great game, Mr. Lunas. Maybe one day I can caddy for you, always been interested in the game of golf." He smiled.

"Really? Well, why didn't you ever say so? My next PGA game, you're going to be my caddy."

"My dad, the golf pro." Jordan smiled.

"Come on son, move the car."

"Ok Dad."

Jordan opened the door and slammed it shut, the van shook from the slam, which seemed louder than it should have been. Brian sat quiet, waited til he saw Jordan and his father walk away.

"Elizabeth, what are we going to do? We can't go to the pool house, his mom's back there."

"I don't know, we'll think of something. Erik you can come out now. Brian, I think maybe we can drive the van up the drive to the side of those hedges over there and then maybe wait. Erik can sneak out and crawl to the pool house, the bushes go all way up to it, see? Plus, he said that no one ever uses the pool house. So I think it's the best place for him."

"I know, last time I saw people there was when we had Jordan's surprise sixteenth birthday party. Come on Erik, climb over. But you know Jordan's mom will probably stop and say Hi to us and you know how impatient Erik is. Remember that time at the Strawberry Festival when we all almost got kicked out because he didn't want to wait in line for the Scrambler?"

"Yeah, that was pretty sad." Elizabeth smirked.

"Erik, come on man, the coast is clear." Brian turned around to reach for him but instead, he could see Erik, outside, walking away and down the long driveway.

"Oh crap!!"

Elizabeth turned around.

"Oh no!"

She turned on the van, flung it in reverse and punched the gas.

"Brian, quick! Open the side door, grab him, hurry!"

Out front, Jordan was just pulling out with the Mustang convertible and saw the van speeding in reverse. His father had not yet come out of the garage.

"Hurry Brian!"

"For crying out loud, Elizabeth! Slow down!"

Erik was walking, aimlessly, again in a trance. A passerby was speeding, and Erik had walked out onto Windhorst Road. The car swerved and had just missed him, the driver was blowing the horn madly.

"Stupid teenager!" he screamed.

The van screeched to a halt.

"Erik, get in!"

Erik ignored him.

"Erik!"

Jordan punched the gas and sped out to the street. From his viewpoint, he saw that there was another car coming and it was headed straight at Erik. He blew the horn screaming.

"Q!!"

The on-coming car's driver was busy texting and looked up just seconds before seeing the dark teen.

"ERIK!!"

Screeeeech! THUMP!!

Brian, Elizabeth, and Jordan were in shock to see their friend bounce off the hood of the SUV and fly across the street into the vacant lot.

"No!!!"

Brian jumped out of the van and ran across the street screaming. Jordan screeched his tires and hopped out over the windshield. Elizabeth managed to cross the street still in reverse. The SUV sped off with a nervous driver behind the wheel.

"Hey! You come back here!" Brian screamed pointing at the speeding Hyundai.

Jordan's dad quickly hopped out of his car and ran toward them across the street.

"Jordan?!"

"Oh God, your dad's coming! Where's Erik?!"

"There he is." Jordan pointed, "... quick Brian, get him!"

The van blocked his dad's view which gave Jordan and Brian the few seconds they needed to grab him and shove him back into the van. Erik seemed groggy but not hurt.

"Hurry, Dad's almost here!"

Brian hopped back in the van, Elizabeth threw a beach towel at him, Brian covered Erik with it and then sat on him. Jordan's dad rushed to the side of the van where Jordan had approached the door.

"Jordan!? Son!"

"Uh Dad, I uh...?"

"Man, I thought I got those brakes fixed! Thank God you're not hurt!"

"Huh?"

"The brakes, your mom told me that the brakes were slipping on the Mustang, that's why we've left it in the garage. The mechanic said it was fixed, but seeing you lose control like that, it's obvious that he didn't fix it! I'll be calling him in a few minutes. Are you ok, son? Are you guys all ok?"

"Uh," he turned and looked at Elizabeth, "… yeah Dad… I'm ok. I'm fine, I just…"

Erik moved, trying to shove Brian off of him. Jordan's dad saw Brian jerk to the left then shove himself back down.

"You ok Brian?"

"Yes sir, Mr. Lunas, uh… gas."

Then he let out a loud burp.

"*BROOAAUKK*! Oh man, excuse me sir, it must have been those oatmeal raisin muffins that Elizabeth made."

"Uh… yeah."

She frowned at him.

"Dad, you go to the golf thing, I'll talk to Mike the mechanic about the brakes."

"Son…"

"No, really Dad, just go. Don't worry about it, I'm fine."

He looked around at the two friends, and Brian who kept moving up and down in the back of the van.

"Really Dad. I'm ok. Don't miss the tournament; we can bring the car back to the garage."

"Well, ok. And Brian, get something for that gas, will ya?"

"Right away Mr. Lunas."

"Ok, see you son. In fact, don't touch that Mustang, leave it where it is. I'll call a tow truck and they'll haul it over to Mike's shop. I just don't wanna take a chance."

"Ok Dad."

He turned to walk back to his BMW and Erik motioned to get up. Then he turned back to the van. Brian slammed Erik's head back on the van floor.

Thunk!

"Ow!"

He looked at Brian.

"Brian, are you sure you're ok?"

"Never felt better, sir." He fidgeted nervously.

"Uh ok... Jordan. Make sure you leave the key in the glovebox."

"Ok Dad."

Elizabeth was holding in a scream, she knew how impatient Erik was, he would burst any second.

"Ok, see ya kids."

"Bye, Mr. Lunas."

He finally walked away.

"Whew."

Brian got up and pulled the towel off.

"Geez Brian, get off me! And why'd you have to slam my head on the floor, good thing I'm dead or I'd have a concussion!"

"Dude you almost got us busted! Why were you walking out in the street?"

"Wait, I was?"

"Yes Erik, you were!" Elizabeth said pointing at him.

"I don't even remember, well wait – I know I felt this…thing inside, like a voice, told me to follow…"

"Follow what?"

"I don't ask questions!"

"That's new." Jordan chuckled.

"How so?"

"It asked him to follow, you've never been a follower."

"Ok well right now guys, we still need to figure out how we're going to get Erik in the pool house. Your mom is back there, Jordan."

"Yeah."

A van drove up the driveway and stopped just behind Elizabeth's.

"Problem solved." Jordan smiled.

"How?"

"That's our gardener, Mr. Edwards, and he has new a helper today." He smiled.

Within minutes, Elizabeth, Jordan and Brian were walking out in the backyard by the pool.

"Hi, Mom!"

"Jordan. Oh hello, Elizabeth, Brian."

"We're going to hang out at the pool house Mom."

"Ok, Honey."

"Mrs. Lunas, hi."

It was the gardener, he walked into the back yard with two helpers, one of them, the thinner, younger looking one was holding a bag of fertilizer over his face. Mr. Edwards stopped and held a small conversation with her while the young helper dropped the bag near the fence and quickly made his way to the pool house. Brian opened the door, and they hopped in.

"Whew."

"Ok, that was close. So, we need to make a plan. First we need to know why you keep zoning out Erik, because you walking off like you do is not going to look good when most people around here were at your funeral. That's all you need is to spread panic."

"Yeah, Q."

"It's a shame Mrs. Lunas, you know?" the voice came from outside the door. It was the gardener's voice; they had walked by the pool house and were right by the window. Elizabeth put her finger to her mouth.

"Shh."

"... I know John, he was such a young vibrant kid, you know, everyone liked him. He was my son's best friend, it's just sad."

"Well on the way here I heard on the radio that they think the robbers struck again. I guess they have some kinda plan worked out in their robberies, the police just can't catch them. They're a couple of smooth criminals if you ask me."

"Where did they rob this time?" she asked.

"Over in Valrico, they know it's the same guys. Cops are going to be all over it. I wouldn't drive in that direction on your way out, Ma'am."

"Valrico?" Erik said.

"Shhh!" Brian covered his mouth.

"Thank you John," she smiled, "... uh what happened to that new help of yours? I thought I saw two helpers?" she looked around.

"Oh, you know those youngsters." he chuckled.

She patted him on the back and then walked away.

"Jordan Honey, I'm leaving." She called out.

"Bye Mom."

"Goodbye Mrs. Lunas." Brian smiled sticking his head out the door.

She walked away back toward the house, humming to herself. Brian stepped back into the pool house. Erik got up and glanced out of the window. The gardener was working the yard spreading mulch and Erik turned back to his friends. He was in deep thought. All of a sudden, something the gardener said triggered something in his head.

"Valrico… that's where I was supposed to be going… that's where the voice said I needed to…" Erik said it in a whisper, then held back.

"What voice?"

"I don't know Lizzy, I felt this voice inside and it told me to go to Valrico, then I kinda blacked out."

"You didn't black out, you started walking… right out of the van out into the street. Don't you even remember? We didn't even hear you leave the van, dude!"

Jordan turned to Erik, rubbed his chin like he was stuck in thought.

"Q, when you went into your trance thing before that… did you also feel a voice calling you?"

"You mean back at the graveyard? Yeah, I guess, I guess I did…"

"You're being called to your murderers, you see? That's why you're still here." Elizabeth said.

"Whoa."

KNOCK KNOCK!!

The knocking at the door rattled *the Quatro*. Elizabeth pointed at Erik, then at the sofa, then at Brian and at the door. Erik jumped behind the couch; Brian ran to answer the door.

"Uh, who is it?"

"Morgan."

"Whew."

He opened the door; Morgan walked in and was followed by two other teens.

"Whoa!?" Jordan gasped.

"What the..?"

"I stopped to get gas and Christy and Kimmy were there with Christy's Mom, so they came along. I told them I was coming to Jordan's house."

"Morgan we asked you to come alone!" Elizabeth barked.

"No you didn't!"

Elizabeth turned to Brian in disbelief. He hunched his shoulders.

"Well, Elizabeth, we actually *didn't* ask her to come alone, she's right you know." He smiled.

"Geez-a!" she slapped her forehead.

"What's the big deal, Elizabeth?" Kimmy asked, "… what, you don't want us here?"

Brian closed the door, motioned for them to sit on the chairs there. Jordan was shaking his head in a big smile.

"What's the big deal? Is that what you asked, Kimmy?"

Christy got up and got in Elizabeth's face.

"Yes, did I stutter? What's the big deal that Kimmy and I came along?"

"Sit down Christy, and I'll show you what the big deal is. I am going to love this, where's my phone?"

"Why do I have to sit down, Jordan?!"

Morgan walked up to the two of them. They could tell that she knew something was up, she had this strange look in her eye. They knew Morgan too well to think they could hide something from her. She wasn't like most her age.

"Why did you even ask me to come? It's not like we hang out or anything. The only things we have in common are band and Erik."

"Well, we most definitely didn't ask you over for rehearsal, Morgan." Brian chuckled.

"So? Why am I here?"

"Yeah, why are we here?" Christy asked, "… if it isn't band related? And I sure don't see Erik anywhere!"

Elizabeth faced Morgan, then turned to Brian, who turned to Jordan, who was standing behind the couch and motioned his hand up in a quick wave. The girls saw a slow movement from behind the couch, first the clump of dark curly hair, then a familiar dark face with a familiar goofy smile. And he stood full, adjusted his shirt, cracked his neck then slowly waved.

"Hi guys."

Their eyes widened in shock.

"ERIK!?"

"Oh... oh my…"

Christy fell back into Brian's arms.

"Erik!?" Morgan ran to him to grab him in a hug, but then stopped mid-way, pulled back, and composed herself, "… uh, Erik?"

She stared at the ring on his finger; it caught her attention, more so than it did anyone else in the small pool house. And the look of shock on her face was something she tried to hide but couldn't for long in the small building. The pool house was actually a small cement block shack that Jordan's dad had built so they could store pool supplies in the back of, but it was also a small apartment that could be used as a guest house if needed, complete with seating area where some guests attending pool parties could change, chat and freshen up. Jordan had many sleepovers here and *the Quatro* used it as a sort of club house.

But this was no sleepover or a normal *Quatro* chill session. The friends here were in the midst of something totally fresh and new to anything they'd ever experienced before. Kimmy stood shocked; she couldn't speak. She just pointed at him and offered a slow steady nervous hum. Erik walked around the couch to her.

"It's me Kimmy, ha, it's really me." he smiled.

He got closer and kissed her on the cheek.

"Erik?"

"Yes, Kimmy." he smiled.

She took a step back; her expression went from surprise to anger in a split second and she slapped him across the face. He fell back on the couch.

60

"This is the absolute worst prank you have *ever* pulled Erik Jason Quince! I mean, the time you put laxative in my chocolate shake at Steak-N-Shake was bad, or the time you told me to go to Chik-Fil-A that Sunday and I forgot that they were closed on Sundays! Or even that time at Oakfield Lanes when you rigged a bowling pin on wheels and it kept rolling away from the ball, but faking your death... oh this is low, even for you Erik! You are disgusting! And all you jerks were in on it?"

She jumped on him and started smacking him on the chest.

"Kimmy! Kimber! Chill man!" Jordan screamed pulling her off. She was fuming.

Christy was slowly coming to after her faint into Brian's arms.

"This isn't a prank, Kimmy. This is actually real. Erik's back, he's not pulling a prank on you this time."

She stared into Elizabeth's eyes when she said it, then turned to the others in the room, they were nodding. Then her eyes rested on Erik, who was brushing himself off.

"Huh?"

"It's not a prank, this is... this is really happening, honest."

Kimmy walked up to Erik again and he flinched back expecting another slap. She pointed her finger in his face.

"What do you mean this isn't a prank?! If it's no prank, then what - we're staring at a freaking zombie!? What do you think I am, an idiot?"

None of *the Quatro* said anything, then Erik's lips curled up in a wicked, creepy smile.

"Ha, wait," Christy entered, "... for a second there you guys almost had me believing that this is really Erik. Come on who is it? Peter in disguise? Morgan are you in on this?"

Morgan hunched her shoulders. Erik walked up to Christy and Kimmy and took each one of them by the hand, a chill entered their bodies from the hand all the way up to their shoulders in a split second. They looked into Erik's coal-black eyes. He had a dead stare that almost seemed kind of spooky.

"It's really me guys." he smiled, "... serious."

Kimmy yanked her hand away.

"Oh my God, Oh my God... oh my freaking Bobbers!" she raised her hands and formed her two index fingers into a cross.

"Stay back you, you Walking Dead reject! I don't believe it... Erik's a freaking zombie!"

Brian started singing a line from Michael Jackson's *Thriller* and did the moonwalk.

She threw her purse at him.

"Shut up Brian!"

The purse bounced off his chest.

"Ow Kimmy! Why ya wanna trip on me?"

Erik started laughing and walked up to her, of all the friends he had in school, she was the most annoyed by his gags, and Erik was famous for his gags, he would carefully plan out a gag for weeks ahead just to see her cringe, but this time it was no gag, and he just wasn't sure that she was finally accepting that this was real.

She stared at him and went back in her head of the time they had a pool party, right here at Jordan's house and everyone had told her that Erik was with his family in Puerto Rico on vacation. The cement statue standing near the diving board was as old as the house was and they even had a name for him, 'Juan'. Sometimes they'd throw their towels on him to dry. But at that particular pool party, Brian had asked her to get his towel off of Juan and when she walked up to it, it turned and screamed "Arrgh!" at her. She was so petrified that she fell into the pool, clothes and all with the towel in her hand, and it turned out to be Erik, coated with some kind of cement-looking body make-up. He had gone through hours with Jordan, Elizabeth, and Brian to put it on, just to scare her. And her response was worth it that day. Yes, Kimmy knew that Erik would go out of his way to pull a prank, she stared at him.

"Ok, so wait. So… you're dead." She said. It was a statement, but it sounded like a question. He nodded his head.

"But you're still here with us?" Christy added.

He and Brian nodded their heads.

"And uh, weren't we at your funeral?" Kimmy asked.

This time, Erik, Brian, Elizabeth, and Jordan all nodded their heads.

"Uh… ok this is freaky."

"That's why I called you here Morgan." Elizabeth said walking over to the door.

"Me? Uh, why me?" Morgan asked.

She glanced over at Erik, and they shared a stare that no one else there quite understood. She glared at him, her eyes opened for a second as if to ask, "What's going on?" and he just shook his head in a quick gesture, then turned away.

"Well Morgan," Elizabeth answered, then she peeked out the door the gardener was on the other side of the yard, "… Erik is going to stay here in the pool house for now, but he still can't just go out, looking like this, so we need to fix him."

"Whoa, whoa... what do you mean 'fix'?" he asked. He held his fingers out making quotation marks.

"Christy, you have your makeup kit on you?"

"Yep."

"Kimmy?"

She nodded her head.

"Ok Erik, sit down."

"Whoa... whoa man, you ain't putting makeup on me! Who do you think I am, Michael Jackson?"

"*Hee hee hee…*" Brian sang.

"Erik, sit down."

"No, Morgan."

Brian grabbed Erik by the shoulder and shoved him back into the seat. The girls cornered him.

"This should be interesting." Jordan chuckled.

"Hey, come on man... I ain't puttin' no make-up on!" he screamed.

"Shut up, dead boy." Elizabeth ordered.

"Yo Brian, let's go up to the house and get some snacks." Jordan walked over and opened the door.

"Jordan, does your mom have any wigs?" Christy called out.

"I doubt it, but I'll check. You guys want popcorn or something?"

The girls nodded. The two friends left the pool house with Erik squirming in his seat.

"Sit still, Q!" Christy said, she punched him on the arm.

"Ow!"

CHAPTER 6

The graveyard was vast. To think that hundreds if not thousands of dead bodies lay here just six feet under the ground was a thought to be reckoned with. But it was peaceful, quiet, and empty except for a family that had just left from the south lawn of Hillsboro Memorial Cemetery. They were headed toward Brandon Boulevard and merging into traffic. Over on the fresh grave of Erik Jason Quince, a shadow slowly appeared. It covered the headstone and towered next to the small oak tree nearby. There was an eerie presence about this shadow, it wasn't from a tree or a headstone, something cast the shadow, but the originator could not be seen. The words on the tombstone were slowly read by the visitor and repeated in a low, gravel, baritone voice.

"*'Erik J. Quince, rest in peace, we love you son.'* Rest in peace… really?" it grunted in what sounded like a chuckle. Then the shadow slowly faded off.

It was a normal day for a Sunday afternoon in sunny Brandon, Florida. Traffic in this section was thick as usual for a weekend; the mall entrance was just yards away. Brandon was a community that could almost be incorporated into its own city. There was an honorary Mayor, fire stations and a history dating back to the late 1800's back when it was called New Hope. The census claimed over a hundred thousand Brandon residents. It hosts the Hillsborough County fair every year and due to the climate was a regular stop for visitors. The Florida sun was glaring as was normal, and drivers were used to donning shades up and down this long stretch of road.

Back at the pool house, a pair of shades was in Christy's hand and was the final touch on their hard work. Jordan and Brian walked in with a tray of pizza rolls and a sour cream and onions Pringles canister. Jordan had a wig in his left hand, tossed it at Kimmy.

"It was in a donation box in the hallway, Mom does a lot of charity work."

Morgan stood close and watched the transformation in a weird smile. The girls' backs were to the boys when Elizabeth put the short dirty blonde wig on their subject, then snipped here, there, combed and tucked.

"What do you think, girls?" Elizabeth smiled.

"Ahh, a masterpiece." Kimmy smiled back.

They slowly backed away and Erik stood, smirking in disgust. Jordan and Brian first gasped in shock, then turned to each other and burst out laughing.

"Hey, what's so funny man! Give me a mirror or something somebody!" Erik protested.

"Dude, you look like that guy… what's his name Jordan? From Back to The Future?'

"Marty McFly!"

"Yeah, ha, ha, ha!" the two friends were laughing it up and Erik was not amused, at all.

Christy handed him a mirror.

"Wha..? Dude! I look like a white guy!"

"We're going to call him... Marty!"

"Ok why do I have to look like this, guys?"

"Because you're going to school with us, that's why, Marty."

"School? Oh no I'm not!"

"Oh yes you are! You can't stay here all day and then zone out and start wandering all over Brandon. You'd cause widespread panic!" Elizabeth said.

"Aw man…"

Christy grabbed a pizza roll and popped it in her mouth.

"Mm pepperoni, yummy, Erik want one?"

"Uh, pass."

"Pass? You're going to pass… on food? Are you guys sure this is Erik?"

"Pretty much." Brian smiled.

"Yes that's Erik." Morgan said folding her arms, she never stopped her stare into him.

"I'm not sure about this Christy," he said, "… and I don't care what they show on TV and movies, but I'm not sure that dead people eat. I don't feel hunger."

"Wow that's a good one, Erik doesn't eat! Erik the human vacuum."

"His name is Marty, Kimmy."

"Oh yeah, Marty. And uh, how are we supposed to get Marty into school? Don't you need paperwork or something?"

"Don't forget your paperwork." Jordan and Brian said mocking the famous line off the movie *Monsters Inc*. Then they started laughing again.

"Geez-a. Get serious guys*!"*

"I bet Mrs. Andrews can help." Morgan said.

"Mrs. Andrews? The A.P. economics teacher? Are you nuts?"

"No Brian, she told me once that Erik reminded her of her little brother."

"Well, we can't tell her that Erik, uh Marty here is a zombie, Morgan!"

"I'm not a zombie already!"

"Says the walking dead guy." Jordan chuckled.

"Geez! Do I really have to go around looking like this? This sucks!"

"Yes Marty!" Elizabeth chopped.

"Well at least I don't look like myself, maybe I can stop by the house and see Mom and Dad."

"No Erik! You can't go to your house! Your parents aren't in the mood to see another teenager right now."

"Why?"

"Your mom blames us for your death, we told you, man, she hates us!"

"Oh, yeah, yeah..."

"So how do we do this then, guys?" Morgan asked, she was walking toward the door.

"I'm going to see Mrs. Andrews first thing tomorrow morning, and we have band practice tomorrow after school, so Erik... uh, Marty, you have to come to school with us." Elizabeth said.

"Man, even dead I have to go to school? That sucks!"

"Get over it buddy, you're still a student at old Victoria High... home of the Wasps." Brian smiled.

Morgan glanced at his ring again which was flashing off and on in its weird amber hue. It seemed to take a life of its own at times.

Outside, unknown to the friends, the shadow from the cemetery crept onto the Lunas property. The entity stood at the edge of the huge driveway and looked around, it was on a mission, it had a target to find and the target was now in makeup, but it could feel Erik, it just didn't know exactly where he was. It cast a shadow but there was no being, no body... just a dark shade of its form that cast in the sunlight that grew as it floated over the driveway. As it passed over the lawn, grass blades wilted and died. The form of a hand came into shape and waved over Jordan's mom's prize flowerbed, and they curled over dead.

Back in the pool house, the door was left opened. Morgan had left the friends talking and went to her car on the other side of the house. She hadn't said much the whole time they were there; it was more like she was studying the whole situation. Kimmy and Christy were going to meet her at the car after a final goodbye to *the Quatro*.

"Ok guys, we're going back home, see ya in school tomorrow. Christy, don't forget your makeup kit? Morgan's probably at the car by now. See you Elizabeth."

"Man Elizabeth, I sure hope this works." Christy smiled.

"Me too. Right now, it's all we've got. We definitely can't leave Erik alone for a second."

"Yeah," Jordan added, "… or he'll go into one of his hypnotic states and…"

Erik stood up, his eyes were fixated outside. He walked around Kimmy and started for the door.

"Erik?"

He didn't answer.

"Oh no, not again!" Brian screamed.

"Q, come back in here!" Jordan and Kimmy called together.

They both grabbed his stone-cold arm, but he was dragging both of them outside. Their forcing him back with all their strength had no physical effect on him, where he gained this new strength was something totally new to them.

"Erik!" Elizabeth ran outside and blocked him.

Staring at him, she saw that it seemed his eyes were fixed on something, and she turned around and she saw the dark shadow slowly take shape while it floated around the corner of the house.

"Guys!?" she screamed.

They all ran to the door, Brian was first to glance out.

"W-w-what the heck is *that* thing?"

He pointed out, all of them stared at it. Erik kept walking toward it, like he was drawn to it like a magnet. The light on his ring started glowing brighter.

"Erik, stop!!" Jordan yelled.

Erik didn't even seem to hear him, or he was ignoring him, they weren't sure. The form started changing into a humanoid shape of some kind, the shape of a tall man in a black cloak, and boney zombie-like hands stretched out, like they were beckoning the teenaged dark Cuban toward it. The friends all felt helpless.

"Erik!!!" Elizabeth's screams didn't faze him.

Then out of nowhere, the screeching of tires made all heads turn. The Jeep Liberty burned out from the side of the house and sped by the dark cloaked figure and toward the friends.

"Morgan! Geez, who does she think she is... the Stig?"

"Shove Erik in the car, hurry!" she screamed.

Brian was there first, he opened the door, the girls shoved Erik in the back seat and then everyone, but Elizabeth and Jordan hopped in.

"Elizabeth, meet us at Mariposa's parking lot!" Morgan screamed.

The car burned out, ruining landscaping all the way out. The being rose in anger and let out a heart-wrenching scream.

"Noooooo!"

The air around them quickly started to smell like rotted meat, and then the shadow vanished after the deep frustrated moan reverberated around the back yard.

"Come on Elizabeth, let's skip!"

The two remaining friends ran to her van.

Morgan's car hopped out over the lawn down to the street and burned rubber down Windhorst Road.

"Erik, what *was* that thing back there?" Kimmy yelled.

Erik was dazed.

"Huh?"

"What was that, that thing? The Grim Reaper?" she asked.

She was sitting in the back seat. Erik sat in back between her and Christy and he still was waking up from the whole thing. Brian had turned around.

"Yeah man? What's going on, why do you go into these trances?"

"I... I..."

"Yeah Erik, they told me about it but I didn't believe it till I just saw it!" Christy added, "... what the heck is going on man!"

"I... uh..."

"He doesn't know." Morgan said still speeding down the road. Her eyes were fixed in front of her on the traffic.

"Huh?"

"He can't control it, he doesn't feel when it happens and he probably doesn't have a lot of time left."

"Morgan what are you talking about?" Brian barked.

She glanced up into the rear-view mirror at Erik and said nothing else.

The friends all sat outside at their favorite eatery and bakery, Mariposa's. They picked the outdoor picnic tables and huddled around. Elizabeth reached over and pulled Erik's wig down a little lower over his forehead. It wasn't too hot, but the sun was out. Erik didn't even break a sweat which was the total opposite of when he was alive, if he was in the sun, he'd start sweating. He sat there, across from Elizabeth, still in makeup and wig, and looked out across the street, where it happened, his death. Jordan and Brian walked out of the eatery with a Cuban sandwich they were going to split. Morgan was just in the middle of explaining to them why this was happening, but Elizabeth kept stopping her and asking questions.

"Man, you guys are always eating," Elizabeth said shaking her head at Jordan, "... so what were you saying, Morgan? He cheated death?"

Morgan wasn't a talker mostly, and she didn't like sharing too much with people, she had her reasons. But this time it was obvious to them that she knew something that no one else did – so unfortunately all attention was on her.

"Yes, Erik cheated death, a messenger has been sent to get him, he has to bring him back. He's not going to stop until he gets him. The good thing is that Erik has to be in his grasp to go, he can't magically take him. He has to physically grab him."

"You mean that spooky shadow-looking thing we saw at Jordan's?"

"Yes Brian, that spooky shadow is an Agent of Death. He has no spiritual power over life or death, but his job is to bring Erik back. So, he does have the power to pull Erik from inside toward him, totally against his will. Well, if he had a will…"

"The trances…" Erik whispered.

"Yep. And that ring… the ring is a major player to this whole thing; it has something to do with it. You can't take it off, can you Erik?"

He reached over with his other hand and tried, it wouldn't budge, but it was glowing like mad.

"It's like glued to me."

"Yeah, that's the one thing I'm still trying to figure out. How does it fuse itself to you? Dad never explained that part."

"Uh Morgan, there's one thing I think all of us need to understand though," Christy asked.

"What?"

"Well, exactly *how* do you know about this stuff?" she asked edging up on the table.

She looked around at each of them. It was obvious that she didn't really want to share any more information. She'd felt like she had already told them more than they needed to know as it was. Morgan never felt comfortable with people her age, she always seemed an older soul. She was different, set apart, but Erik helped bring her out of it many times since elementary school.

She let out a nervous breath and stared around at the friends, they all had her undivided attention.

"Do you guys know what my dad does for a living?" she asked.

"Nope," Jordan said chewing on his sandwich.

"Good why don't we keep it like that." she smiled.

"What is he, a funeral home director? Geez."

"No Christy… let's just say I kinda know about death."

76

"I'd say that's kinda obvious." Jordan smirked, making quotation marks with his fingers in the air when he said the word "kinda".

"Ok, so then if what you say is true, how do we save Erik?"

"Brian, we can't save him. He's dead and he has to go back, he's here for a reason and we have to find out why or this thing isn't going to stop till it can get him. And by the way, the thing doesn't care if you have a mission Erik, as far as he's concerned, he's like the Terminator. He has one job, one goal... to bring you back to death's door."

"I don't wanna die," Erik whined.

"*You're already dead!*" everyone at the table screamed.

"Oh... yeah, yeah."

"Did you hear?" the voice was from an older person just feet away from them and startled a couple of them.

All the friends at the table turned. The woman had just walked out of her parked car and was walking into Mariposa's.

"They just announced on the radio that one of the bank robbers from here last week was apprehended in Valrico, in the middle of a robbery, he fell into some kind of shock. He's in police custody now; they say he looks like he saw a ghost. That poor child who was killed across the street last week is probably overjoyed in his grave, rest his soul. At least one of those criminals was caught."

The woman was talking to the friends at the table and Elizabeth smiled.

"I'm sure he's smiling as we speak, ma'am."

Erik smirked a goofy smile that made Brian chuckle. In makeup and the nicely fitting wig, he looked nothing like his former self.

The woman looked across the street at the white cross that was put there in remembrance of Erik and walked into the establishment. It was Brian who put the cross there.

"Ok that was freaky, he was caught in Valrico and Erik said he felt 'the call' to go to Valrico. I mean it's only down the street about a mile or two but still, that's freaky." Jordan quipped.

"I'm going in to get a cookie, Christy come with me. Morgan, you're creeping me out man." Kimmy got up and Christy followed her into the bakery.

"Dude, we have to find out what she means about the bank robber going into shock and…"

Jordan was chewing his last piece of sandwich when he turned to Erik and the familiar blank stare came over his face.

"Oh no."

Morgan stood up and looked down the parking lot, from the look on her face, it was obvious that she saw something but no one else there, except Erik saw it too.

"Elizabeth, we have to go, now!" she slammed her hand on the table.

Brian and Jordan didn't think twice, they each grabbed Erik's arm on either side and threw him in the van.

"What's happening!?" Elizabeth screamed fumbling for her keys.

"They found us, hurry!"

"Who found us Morgan!?" Jordan was last to get in and slammed the door.

"Go go go!!!"

Elizabeth shoved it into drive and the Honda Odyssey minivan screeched out of the parking lot and sped down Robertson Street. Morgan jumped to the back of the van and peered out of the window.

"Crap Elizabeth, hurry! Geez this can't be happening; *this can't be happening!*" Morgan screamed.

She reached the intersection of Kings Avenue and took a hard left and headed North. She flew into the street like a speed demon.

"Morgan who's after us? I don't see anything!" Elizabeth screamed looking through the rear-view mirror.

"Just go! Beat it!"

Erik started moaning, it was like a mixture of pain and laughter, and the moan came from deep within, and all of a sudden it started to smell in the van, it was a stench that caused some of them to almost gag, Brian held his nose.

Jordan opened the window and stuck his face out.

Back at Mariposa's, the door opened, and Christy and Kimmy walked out with two bags full of baked goods.

"Ok guys, we got something for every… *hey!?* "

"They ditched us! *Oh that Erik*, wait till I get my hands on him! You *know* he was up to this! He's the king of ditching people! I'm going to choke him Christy, do you hear me!?!" Kimmy fumed.

Elizabeth took a right on Brandon Boulevard and sped east. Erik was still moaning.

"Erik what is that smell, a zombie fart?"

"No," Morgan said, "… it's the smell of death."

"He's already dead!" Brian screamed.

"Well then the smell is catching up to him." Jordan uttered; his face was still out the window.

Elizabeth glared back in the rear-view mirror, adjusted it to see Erik's full face.

"Erik what's going on? Who's after you? Why are they after you!? Why do you keep zoning out!?"

"Aw man I'm about to throw up my sandwich!" Jordan whined.

Erik was still moaning, and he didn't even bother to answer her. He looked like he wasn't feeling too well.

"Uh Erik, do zombie's throw up?" Brian asked, "… because I sure don't wanna know what *that* smells like!"

"I'm not a zombie, man!" he said to his best friend.

Elizabeth turned on Sadie Street and rushed into the parking lot of the park there. She parked way in back near the railroad tracks, coincidentally as a train was whizzing by. It was normally a quiet spot where people would park their cars to read or eat lunch or something. The van's ignition was shut off and they all let out a sigh of relief.

Elizabeth threw her hair back in a frustrated shove with her hand and turned to them in her seat.

"Morgan, are they still back there, whoever they are?"

"No Elizabeth, they, I think they're gone."

"Ok good," she wiped her brow, "… now, will somebody *please* tell me what's going on!?" she screamed punching her seat.

Morgan turned to Erik. He held up his face so they were looking into each other's eyes.

"Erik, when you passed over, what happened? You saw a light, you were attracted to it, what happened after that? That light is almost impossible to walk away from, it's your destiny."

"I told you guys already man."

"No, I feel like there's something else you haven't told us, you have Agents of Death after you Erik, why? What did you do?!"

"Agents of Death? Morgan what are you talking about? You said that before… Agent of Death, who… what is it?" Brian asked.

Morgan turned to Brian but wasn't about to elaborate.

"Morgan, you better tell them the truth about you, I think it's time." Erik shrugged.

She breathed in, let out a long sigh. Then she looked around the van, all eyes were on her. Erik was staring out the window into the park. Morgan's eyes rested on Elizabeth.

"Well?"

Morgan wasn't comfortable with this, but she was on the spot. She didn't even know where to start, she smiled at her herself, thinking maybe she could just lie, give them something completely bogus and off the wall, but…

"Ok, but I'm telling you, you guys won't believe it."

"Try us."

She turned to Jordan when he said that, he had rested his face on his hands as he stared at her and smiled.

"Ok, well here goes… My dad is, well you guys met my Dad at the football games when we play with the band, right? Remember?"

"Yeah, your dad loves hotdogs." Brian smiled.

"With sauerkraut," Jordan added.

"So, what about your dad, Morgan?"

Elizabeth wanted her to get straight to the point and stop stalling. She could tell that the blonde was beating around the bush.

"Well, you see...my dad... he uh, well he is a Reconciler. There, I said it. Can we go now?"

They all stared around in the van, then all eyes turned to Erik who was waving his hand in a circular motion in the air signaling to Morgan that she needed to go on with the story. He knew his friends; they weren't just going to let it go with that statement.

"Wow Morgan," Brian smiled, "... I would have never guessed that. Did you say Reconciler? Man that's awesome, isn't it guys? He's a Reconciler... so what the heck is a Reconciler?"

"He uh... well, he kinda sees dead people, Brian. There, can we go now?"

Silence.

This was the point, they were either going to laugh at her, or wait to hear more. She waited for a sign; she was visibly uncomfortable about this, wiping her forehead of sweat that wasn't even there.

"Uh, yeah ok... and my Dad can fly a plane, Morgan. Let me guess – your dad's a pilot too, huh?" Jordan joked.

"Actually, she's serious Jordan." Erik quipped.

Jordan frowned in curiosity. "Oh... ok."

"Ok wait, wait so you're saying that your dad is what – a medium or something?"

"No, Elizabeth, we don't use the term *medium*. He releases spirits into the afterlife."

"Uh, doesn't that happen normally, like when you die?"

"If it did Jordan, would Erik be sitting in the van with us?" she asked.

"Ok, uh… and how does one go into the releasing spirits into the afterlife business?" Brian smirked, "… is there like a special school for this or something? Death College, University of The Tomb or something?"

"Institute of Deceased Learning?" Jordan started laughing.

"See I knew it would be useless telling you guys. That's why I don't talk to anyone about it, no one but Erik knows."

Elizabeth punched both of them on the arm.

"Ow man!"

"So uh, do *you* see dead people too, Morgan?"

She turned to Elizabeth and held on to her answer. She thought back to that first night at band camp when the camp counselor was telling the story about the battle between the Confederate and Union soldiers. The counselor was just re-telling a tale that was repeated at that camp every year, but what she didn't know was that it was real, it wasn't just a myth or fable, it was a legend, it was true.

And she didn't know that Morgan was actually looking right at them as they crawled out of the dense, dark woods surrounding the camp. No, the camp counselor Miss Bone had no earthly idea that those she was recounting the story about were standing right there surrounding the whole campfire. Had it been a planned ambush during a war, the kids would have been massacred. One of them was sizing up Xavier's head with *his* head for a perfect fit. Xavier couldn't even feel the withered hands with dried blood that were carefully cupping his shaved scalp, neck and cheeks. Another one was drawing a line across the back of Matthew's neck with his rusted dagger. The only thing that stopped them from doing anything was that the commander, Captain Elijah Oliver, his troops called him Captain E-O for short, stood right there unscathed in the middle of the fire and was staring at Morgan. He knew she could see him; she tried not looking but he was a very overpowering presence in his full Union Blue officer's uniform. He drew his sword and pointed it at her.

"She is a Reconciler!" he barked at his troops in scathing rage. Though he was a Northerner, he had a Southern twang in his gravel voice.

All the soldiers turned to her and stared. He raised his sword and swung it in the air in fury; the angry swishing sound of the sharp metal blade made her blink and the birds that were close by all shuddered, flapped their wings, and took off in flight, frightful of the deadly invisible ghoul that stood in the fire.

Morgan held in her breath and her tears, she couldn't say anything that night and it was killing her inside. The kids all jumped at the sound of the birds, some screamed, and some of them got up and ran back to their cabins leaving *s'mores* and skewers with marshmallows on the dry ground. And Counselor Bone was right on time with her delivery...

"That was the ghost of Captain Elijah Oliver, he called off the birds so there'd be no witnesses! Hurry! Run! Save yourselves!"

The kids dashed off screaming to their cabins. Morgan sat there staring at the counselor as she smiled, then at the soldier in the fire, who descended into the flame after a frightful roar. She'd never forget that night.

She blinked once, twice... then turned in the van and stared at Erik.

"Well?' Elizabeth asked.

"Huh? What?" Morgan replied in a daze.

"Yes Lizzy, she *does* see dead people." Erik said. He sat up in the seat and looked around, "... she can do the same thing her Dad can do."

"Whoa, this is heavy." Brian smiled.

"So, you saw something chasing us, why isn't it still chasing us?"

"Because they were called off." Morgan told Elizabeth.

"Called off by whom? And what is an Agent of Death?"

Morgan sat glancing around in the van. She had their full attention now and she didn't want it. She never felt comfortable with her gift.

"Come on Morgan, just tell them." Erik said, "… get it over with. They're going to have to know, they're all involved now."

She covered her face in her hands and started talking without looking at any of them.

"When you die, your spirit leaves your body, you get claimed, then you go. I don't mean to step on anybody's beliefs here, in fact I don't care what you believe, this is what I know."

She looked around, none of them even blinked, she had them floored already. She stuck both her hands out and with her left hand she waved it and said,

"So, Erik either didn't get claimed," then with her right she lowered it and said, "… or he ignored the call. If he ignored the call, then they're after him to bring him back."

"Back… where?"

"Back to where he's supposed to be Brian, dead."

"I'm already dead."

"Yes Erik and something stopped you, you can't just ignore the call, it's overpowering. If it wasn't we'd have corpses walking all over the place. So something or someone else was there when you were soaking in the light."

Morgan looked at Erik, he was still with the wig and makeup on. He dodged her eyes as much as he could. She squinted at him accusingly, then exhaled in frustration.

"That ring on your finger, the glowing gem - that's a Parting Stone. It gets put on those who don't pass over. Well, actually the truth is that it gets *created* as you pass from life to death. That metal, or what looks like gold is actually fragments of your own bones and minerals from your body. The stone... is actually formed from your blood. It's hardened by '*the light*' into a gem. That gem is the beacon that the agents of death can see; they feel it, like a vibrating signal through the air. Your life source is in it. You can't hide from them for long, it's impossible. They'll always find you. It's like the beam of a lighthouse in a fog. But the ring is only formed on those who stray from the light, who ignore the call. So again when you were going to pass over, Erik, you ignored didn't you?"

"He ignored?"

"Well, he is known in school for getting in trouble for not following rules, that's why he's in Principal Diriscall's office all the time."

They all turned to him. Jordan folded his arms.

"Hey I wasn't ready! Somebody killed me, I wanted to get them before I had to go."

"You can't do that Erik!"

"Obviously Morgan, he can." Elizabeth said, "… he did."

"Erik, the Agents won't stop until they get you, nothing can stop them. They're the Agents of Death. The whole world is their playground, you can't hide from them. And it won't be a pretty picture, you cheated death."

"I didn't cheat, I'll die, I'll go! I just want the guys that did this to me to get caught! Isn't that fair?"

"Dude, you're not Batman, you can't go on a witch hunt."

"I can and I will. And I was hoping I could count on my friends, *the Quatro* to help me but if you won't then I'll do it alone!"

"Erik, you *can't* go alone, as soon as you go into one of your trances, you're done for!" Brian told him.

"I *have* to do this guys, don't you understand?"

They did understand. His friends knew more than probably anyone else. Erik Quince wasn't a quitter, but he was also someone who would set something in his mind and then it became his mantra. Like the time he got in trouble for punching the bully. He made it one of his goals to make sure the faculty knew who the bullies were. He didn't care if he'd be labeled a snitch. Erik wasn't into labels, and his head strong attitude got him into many scuffs with the tough kids. He was always determined, and they knew it.

Elizabeth stared into his eyes.

"Lizzy, I won't rest until I get them."

"Ha, you mean you won't *rest in peace*, get it guys, rest in peace? He's dead, see?" Jordan laughed.

Elizabeth rolled her eyes. Erik didn't budge from his glare into her. He was serious and she knew it. She reached up, took his cold hand.

"Ok Erik, we're with you. Let's do this."

"Yeah, those bank robbers are going to regret they ever messed with *the Quatro*."

They all agreed with Brian.

"Yeah Erik, we're *dying* to help!" Jordan smiled.

Elizabeth smacked him on the forehead.

"Ow, man."

CHAPTER 7

Monday morning came quick. Christy ended up spending the night at Elizabeth's house and they had made plans to pick Jordan up so they could refresh Erik's look. They weren't really sure how well this plan would work out but for the moment it was the best they had and at least it kept him safe from himself and his zoning out. The van parked in the student parking lot, Jordan stepped out, then Christy followed and the familiar red converse of the other passenger stepped out. Erik was in full get-up. He wore one of Jordan's long-sleeved *Back to The Future* Jersey shirts and black skinny jeans.

"Ok Marty," he smiled, "... just act normal. Wait, I'm talking to Erik – so normal don't cut it, uh, just act like someone else... with common sense."

"Bite me man."

Elizabeth faced him and straightened out his belt buckle.

"I emailed Mrs. Andrews last night," she said, "... told her that Jordan's cousin Marty from California was in town and wanted to check our school out, so you get to shadow Jordan and Brian all day."

"We didn't have enough makeup to cover everything Erik, so you have to keep this long-sleeved shirt on."

"His name is Marty, Christy." Elizabeth affirmed.

"Oh yeah... Marty. Ha, shirt is fitting."

Brian ran up to them.

"Hey Eri..." Elizabeth quickly covered his mouth.

"Brian, this is Jordan's cousin from California, remember? His name is *Marty.*"

She stared at him, so he'd remember to follow the plan.

"Yeah, yeah... Marty. What up Marty? How's Doc?"

He put his arm around Erik and smiled. Erik looked very uncomfortable in this get-up, but it was the plan and he had to stick with it. Elizabeth patted him on the back.

"Ok Marty, we have to go to Student Affairs and get you signed in." she smiled.

"Uh... yeah."

"This is weird," Jordan whispered to him, "... everybody here was at your funeral, they'd freak out if they knew it was you, bro."

"Tell me about it."

They walked toward the door to the student affairs office. Christy waved over at Kimmy when she saw her down the hall with Morgan. The two friends ran over to see them.

"Hi Erik," she whispered, "... so do you think you can do this?"

"Do I have a choice?'

"No!" they all said together.

"Geez."

"See ya in class, Marty." They walked off and *the Quatro* strolled into the office.

"May I help you?" was the first response they got.

"Uh hi, uh... Miss uh, anyway. Mrs. Andrews said that my cousin Marty here could get a pass and kinda check out Victoria High today with us? He's in from out of town."

"Yes, she sent an email about it this morning." The lady at the desk replied.

Elizabeth looked at the name tag on her desk, "Miss Warrens." she whispered to herself.

Erik stepped up.

"My, you do look familiar." Miss Warrens said.

The Quatro turned around and stared at each other.

"Well of course he does, he's Jordan's cousin." Brian nervously smiled.

"Oh, yes that must be it, and what is your name young man?"

Jordan elbowed him.

"Oh uh... Marty, Mart*yyyy* Quesada, with a Q." he smiled.

Elizabeth rolled her eyes.

"Ok Marty Quesada, welcome to Victoria High and here is your visitor's badge." She peeled it off and handed it to him.

It stuck on his finger and he pulled it off and slapped it on his chest, then Elizabeth gasped when she noticed that some of his make-up off his finger had come off on the label.

"Uh, thank you ma'am, come on Marty, we need to get to class." She hurried.

The four friends stepped out into the hallway.

"What was that about Lizzy?"

"Look Marty," she whispered, "… don't call me Lizzy, only Erik calls me Lizzy and some makeup came off on that label, *geeez-a* you have to watch your skin, man. And really – 'Quesada with a Q'? You used to do that all the time with your real last name Erik Quince – with a Q. You can't be Erik right now; you have to be Marty, ok? Get with the program for crying out loud!"

"Well, what would Marty do?" he asked.

"Well me being the *Back to The Future* expert that I am, Erik… uh Marty… you have to act cool, and say Daddy-O a lot. You have to have this rock star attitude and ignore Lorraine." Jordan smiled.

"Lorraine who?"

"Lorraine from the movie? Remember he went back in time to his parent's high school, and his mom Lorraine had a crush on him because she didn't know who he was, and…"

"Uh oh guys, here comes Johnny." Brian quipped.

"Johnny who?"

The four turned, it was Johnny Goode, the school bully. He stopped right in front of the four friends.

"Why lookey here, it's *the Quatro*, well not exactly, because one is missing and it seems like you guys have already replaced him, ha ha! Yo, who's the new kid? Dude really? *Back to The Future?* Jordan's lending his clothes out now? What a dweeb. Ha!"

He pointed at the shirt and poked the Delorean.

Johnny Bernard Goode was well known in the hallways of Victoria High, not only as Captain of the football and wrestling teams, but he was also a menace to most of the students. He looked much older than his age and looked like he worked out in his sleep. Standing at six foot two, he was also one of the tallest boys in school, aside from those on the basketball team, who all happen to be his friends. His blonde crew cut and menacing green eyes was a staple in the halls of the Brandon Florida high school, all the students knew him, he made a point of that.

"Hey Moose, back off." Erik said shoving his finger away.

Johnny got closer to him.

"Moose? You know what kid? Since you're new and they probably didn't tell you about me, I'm going to let that one slide. See? I can be a nice guy," he smiled showing his perfect teeth, "...so what say for now I'll just go on this way and why don't you make like a tree and get out of here?"

Brian gulped silently. Elizabeth slid her hand under Erik's arm to pull him away. He flinched it back.

"They didn't have to tell me about you, Daddy-O, your breath says enough." He said.

Johnny stopped in his tracks, turned around and stepped back to him, smiled at the friends, then walked up and cupped Erik's throat in his hand.

"You know that attitude reminds me of a kid that used to go to this school. I stress the *used to* part, you see punk, he ain't here no more, you wanna know what happened to him?" he smiled.

"You breathed on him?" Erik quickly snapped back.

"Ha, that's… that's funny, new kid. I tell you what…. you're about to meet him."

Johnny balled his massive fist and quickly pulled it back. His muscular arm snapped like a jackhammer and he forced his fist to Erik's face with all his might and they all heard the slap… but it wasn't his fist connecting with Erik's jaw, instead it was his fist being caught in the air by Erik's new forceful grip, and the dead cold clamp of his grasp sent a chill quickly throughout the bully's muscular body. He stared into Erik's deep black, dead eyes and for a second saw the glimpse of a skull staring back at him then the quick glisten of blood red pupils. They both stood there for a couple of seconds like an arm-wrestling match gone bad, Johnny's huge fist shook in Erik's grip - then Erik shoved his fist back at him and the bully fell against the lockers in a loud thud. He shook from the force and a loud fart burst out of him.

Brian started fanning the air.

"Whew Johnny, what was that - a McDonald's sausage burrito? With special sauce?! I mean *really!!"*

The friends all laughed and Johnny stood up and grabbed Brian by the shirt.

"Is there trouble over here?!"

The loud forceful voice came from the principal who had just walked out of the student affairs office.

"Brian Hill! Are you getting into a fight?"

"Oh… no, not at all Principal, I'm a lover not a fighter."

Johnny loosened his grip, straightened out Brian's shirt.

"Hi Mrs. Diriscal." He offered in a fake smile.

Elizabeth walked up to the principal.

"Oh, hello Mrs. Diriscall, no, no trouble at all, Johnny was just showing us how *not* to embarrass yourself in front of the color guard squad."

The girls from color guard were walking by. Kelsey and Sara, the squad leaders, fanned their hands.

"Somebody had a sausage burrito." Sara said.

"Yeah, with special sauce." Kelsey giggled.

"Mrs. Diriscall, this is my cousin from California, uh… uh…"

"Marty." Brian smirked.

"Yeah, Marty Quesada, with a Q."

Elizabeth shook her head rolling her eyes.

"Uh, very well, carry on children; Marty, welcome to Victoria High, bell's going to ring any minute."

The Quatro walked away leaving Johnny against the locker fuming.

"I hate it when she calls us *'children'*." Jordan smirked.

Brian ran to his locker tugging Erik behind. As Brian grabbed books, a fellow student walked by and stopped. Her mocha skin and long braided hair caught his eye. She took notice of the new kid.

"Hi." she smiled.

"Well, hi…" Erik smiled back.

"You new here?"

"Why, yes, yes I am." he grinned.

"Marty, we have to go!" Brian said yanking his arm.

"I guess I'll have to catch you later, uh..?"

"Jennifer's my name. I guess we will… in the future, Marty."

Brian got close to Erik to whisper.

"What are you doing bro!? You can't date anyone. Love is out of the question!"

Erik watched her walk away, raised his eyebrow, and sighed. "She's out of my life."

"Bro, the power of love is a curious thing, now let's go!" Brian grabbed his collar.

They walked down the hall. Erik was used to high fives and beckons of "Yo Q!" But he got none today. Even Pierce and Joshua walked by him without noticing him. This was something new he'd have to get used to.

The two friends went into the classroom, Advanced Placement American History. He made it to his seat just as the bell rang and the teacher stood at the door checking for stragglers. She was known as a strict teacher to some students, and to others, she was referred to as the *Empress of The Universe* because she had a regal air about her, but she also was very fair. She left the door half open and walked to the massive wooden desk, staring out at the students as they scrambled to their seats.

Erik stared up at her and quickly recognized her as a slow frown overcame his face. Hispanic with a natural tan, she had curly black hair that almost looked frizzy enough to be combed out into an afro; she offered her famous steady smile as the last of the students walked in. Some called it her 'shark stare'.

"Oh snap, this is Miss Valentine, dude she hates me." Erik whispered to Brian from behind.

"Well she doesn't hate Marty right? Now chill dude."

"Ok class, we need to get right into where we left off. School testing is coming and we need serious cramming, so uh…"

99

She was already walking through the aisle of desks and came upon Brian. She stopped and looked at Erik behind him, cocked her head.

"Excuse me, are you new?"

"Uh…"

"Yes ma'am, he is, Miss Valentine, he's Jordan Luna's cousin Marty from California. He's visiting and may start coming here. Cool huh?"

"Oh, I see, Marty from California. You know, I can't help but think that I have seen you before somewhere. Have we met?"

Erik didn't want to look her in the eyes.

"N…no ma'am, not unless you've been to California."

"I *have* been to California; I was in the military before I became a teacher… now where in California are you from?"

"Uh… Hill Valley?"

"*Hmm.*" She rubbed her olive toned chin, "… nope never been there. Well welcome to Victoria High, home of the Wasps."

She reached out her hand and he stretched his out and saw the spot from the label, then he yanked his hand back, covered his mouth and faked a sneeze. Then he stretched out his hand again. She chose not to shake. He knew she would.

"Ok class, so the Seminole Wars in Florida, it was a famous war in our state that they don't talk about much, though I have to admit, I didn't like the outcome of that war. The Seminoles were here before we were. Now, who can tell me what famous General and later U.S. President led the battle against the Seminole Indians here in the Sunshine State?"

Hands went up, but she turned to Erik.

"Marty?"

"Who, me?"

She nodded her head, folded her arms.

"Coming from California I might not expect you to know this, but I do love to challenge my students. Would you like to take a guess? What was the famous General's name?"

"Uh…" he looked up at Brian, who was sitting behind where she stood.

Brian used his index and middle fingers in the form of human legs on his desk and faked the moonwalk across the top of his textbook.

"Uh… Jackson?" Erik curiously shrugged.

"That would be correct, General Andrew Jackson, who incidentally was Florida's first governor. Very good Marty, now class let's open up to chapter fifteen."

Erik breathed out a sigh of relief; Brian gave him an *ok* sign. Erik had been in Miss Valentine's before, just it wasn't in first period and he looked around the classroom at the students, most of whom he knew at least by face. Michelle was sitting right next to him, she was another friend in band, and so was Peter to the left of him and Guillermo in back of him. Michelle had a black armband on her bicep. He hadn't noticed it, but as he looked around, everyone had one, including Brian.

"Excuse me, Michelle, what's the black armband for? Where'd you get it?" he whispered.

She turned to him.

"How do you know my name?"

"Uh, Brian, told me? Yeah."

"Oh, well we're wearing these because…"

"Excuse me you two? I don't see how you can hear what I'm saying when you're talking to each other. Would you like to share this little confabulation of yours with the rest of the class?"

"Sorry Miss Valentine," Michelle offered, pushing her dark blonde hair from her eyes, "… uh the new kid asked me about the armbands and I was explaining."

"Oh…"

Erik looked around; everyone had one on, including the teacher. She walked up to him.

"Marty, didn't your cousin tell you about Erik Quince?"

It was rare that he heard his last name pronounced the way it was supposed to be pronounced. Miss Valentine was Hispanic and she said it the way it was supposed to be said. Everyone else said it in an American accent, pronouncing it 'KEEN-say', though in writing it looked like "kwinse". Quince meant 'fifteen' in Spanish.

"Uh… Erik who?" he asked. He rolled his eyes over to Brian, he really wanted to look like he didn't know anything but it was hard.

"Erik Jason Quince was a senior here at Victoria High who met an untimely death last week here in Brandon. The entire school is honoring him by wearing these bands, would you like one? See they have a purple letter Q on it, Q was his nickname."

"Erik was very special," Michelle said.

The entire class agreed in grunts and nods.

"Oh, I don't mean any disrespect, but aren't you guys only honoring him because he's dead? Did any of you even know him? Or talk to him? Hang out with him, aside from Brian here? You probably didn't even know the guy."

"How dare you!?" screamed another student from across the room. She got up stormed over to his desk and faced him, pointing her finger at his nose.

"You are new here, punk! You didn't even *know* Erik, we did! You take that back, jerk!"

"Maya, calm down." Brian said.

"Hey, I was just asking a question. Everybody in school's wearing something to honor someone they didn't even know. I don't get that. I'm a big fan of the TV show '*Fresh Prince of Bell Air*'. When James Avery the actor who played Uncle Phil died, I didn't wear an arm band, and I loved the guy!"

"Well, that's what separates you California people from us Floridians!" she stormed back to her seat.

"Marty, actually a lot of people knew Erik. True they probably weren't as close to him as Brian here was or the others in *the Quatro*, but we all knew him."

"Ok, I'm sorry. I just... thought it was weird, sorry guys."

Brian was tapping him under the desk on his foot, hoping he would just shut up for the duration of the class.

"Ok class, back to the Seminole war..." the teacher said.

CHAPTER 8

Lunch. The cafeteria was full. Erik had his fill of Victoria High, the second, third, and fourth periods went smoothly, as long as he kept his mouth shut and luckily each of those classes, he had one of *the Quatro* with him and in fourth period he had Brian again. By the time it got to lunch hour, didn't even think about it, he wasn't hungry. And that bothered him, Erik was known for wolfing down food. *The Quatro* sat at their usual table. Jordan was just opening his milk when he felt someone brush up behind him. It was Morgan, who was followed by Christy and Kimmy.

"Hey guys."

"Hi Morgan, what's up?"

"Well, some girls are asking who the new kid is."

"What new kid?"

"You Erik, duhh!" Christy whispered.

"Oh."

"You didn't get lunch, Eri… uh, Marty?"

"No Kimmy, I don't even feel hunger anymore."

"Yeah, he's a zombie… right now he's thinking about biting into your neck, Christy." Jordan laughed.

"Actually, that's kinda gross." Erik smirked.

Kimmy sat next to him, looked at his face.

"May I help you?" Erik asked.

"I'm checking for splotches, stop being rude Marty."

She pulled out a small compact from her purse and showed him, then started rubbing the spot on his chin. She made it look like she was wiping a piece of food off, though he had no tray or plate in front of him.

"Where have you been all my life?" Erik smiled.

"Dream on, Erik." she shrugged.

"He's not talking to you Kimmy," Brian smiled, "… he's talking to the man in the mirror."

"Yo, new kid!"

They all knew the voice and their faces dropped; it came from just a few feet away. They all turned and saw Johnny approaching with two of his muscle-bound buddies.

"Yo, Back to The Future kid, I'm talking to you."

Erik ignored him.

"Hey Brian, pass me that ketchup pack." Erik whispered.

"Erik, I don't think you need to piss this guy off." Christy said.

"Yeah man, stay low-key, dude." Jordan patted his arm.

Elizabeth stood and faced him, blocking his path to Erik.

"Johnny, why are you bothering him? Why can't you bullies ever just leave people alone, you need the attention or something?",

"You know Elizabeth, I always thought you were kinda cute, maybe I should officially make you my girlfriend, huh guys? She's definitely a PYT."

The other two jocks laughed.

He took hold of Elizabeth's wrist.

"Let me go, Johnny." she said trying to yank out of his grip.

He pointed at Erik from behind.

"Yo, freak, I was talking to you."

Erik slowly stood and turned to him, the smirk on his face unnerved Johnny, usually you faced Johnny with fear in your eyes, no one ever smiled.

"Ok Muscle-throat, what's the deal? You wanna fight me? You have to mark your territory? Isn't that what gorillas do?"

"You trying to take up for her, punk? Face it, the girl is mine."

"You're not what she's looking for," Erik said staring him square in the face, "... she likes humans!"

Jordan slowly rose and stepped back.

"Hey cousin Marty, let's just uh... go, huh?"

"Let me go, Johnny!" Elizabeth kicked him against the shin and he loosened his grip. He rubbed his shin in anger and reached out to her again.

"Why you..."

Erik stepped out; he had the ketchup pack in his palm.

"Hey Moose! I don't think Lizzy's your type, why don't you go find Queen Kong or something?"

The bully pulled back his massive fist and swung out, Erik ducked and the force of the swing caused Johnny to stumble toward his new enemy. He tripped just in time to get shoved back by Erik's elbow, then see Erik's open hand quickly approaching. The smack was loud enough that almost everyone, including Miss Valentine, who was passing by, heard it. What everyone saw after that was a splash of red goo that flew out of the hard slap.

Johnny fell back onto his friends. They caught him, they all thought it was blood and he let out a horrific scream that everyone heard. Miss Valentine reached over, grabbed Erik by the arm, and quickly escorted him to the administration wing. He dropped the flattened ketchup pack on the floor, right at the feet of Jennifer, the girl he had met in the hallway.

"Oh boy, this isn't going to be good," Jordan said.

Minutes later, Erik was sitting across the desk of the Assistant Principal, Ms. Brown. She stared at him, speechless for a few minutes. Jordan and Brian had left the lunchroom and sat outside the office hoping that he wouldn't give himself away. But with Erik's temperament, that wasn't a guarantee.

The assistant Principal tapped her pen on the wooden desk. This wasn't the first time Erik was in this office, he knew it well. From the University of South Florida degree framed on the wall just over her head, to the signed Tom Brady portrait she had on the wall just over a Tampa Bay Buccaneers banner. Yes, Erik was used to this room.

"Marty," she sighed, "… ok you've been here half a day and you've already managed to make your way to my office. Johnny Goode is the star quarterback of our football team, and…"

"Johnny Goode is also a bully, you know that – right?" Erik's face, though still in makeup, showed no sense of respect for her. He still remembered the time he got in trouble for fighting a bully in middle school, and then the time AP Brown contacted his parents when he skipped class with one of the guys. She became the enemy that day – Erik never understood that she really was trying to keep him on the straight and narrow.

"Johnny says you attacked him, I have a cafeteria full of witnesses. Johnny may have his faults, but he is a star athlete…"

"Is that all you care about?" Erik said standing up, "… don't you know he harasses students every day? Don't you know that every kid that sees him walking down the hallway wonders if they're going to be the next one he decides to pick on and you people just act like he's freaking Hollywood?! What happened to the '*no tolerance*' policy?"

"Young man..."

"You know what lady, it's people like you, like all of you who ignore it and swear that we don't tolerate bullying, yet you know who the bullies are and you don't do squat about it. I find it funny that every teacher, every administrator, everybody that works here knows us by name, they know our parents, they know our faults and they know who the bad element is, yet the bad guy always gets protected. Can you explain that to me AP Brown? So he helped win the football game but he also put a black eye on Freshman Tommy – as long as our sports team exceeds everything is ok, right? Well, guess what? I'm not going to stand down to him, and I dare him to touch me! If he approaches me again you will be carrying him away."

"Are you threatening Johnny Bernard Goode?" she stood.

"Wow," he stared at her, "...wow... that's amazing. Defend the bad guy, that's just how it works. I guess that's how it works everywhere. In fact, you know that one remaining guy left that shot me? I bet he *lawyers up* and gets off scot-free... well it won't work that way if I find him first."

"What? What man? Shot whom? What are you talking about Marty?"

"I'm done here."

Erik turned and stormed out of the office. Jordan and Brian were there and heard most of it.

"Eri... uh, Marty? Dude, what's going on?"

"I'm outta here, screw this school man!"

Brian turned to the Assistant Principal, and she shrugged. He turned and chased Erik down the hallway.

Jordan stood there, and turned to the A.P.

"How could you?" then he turned and ran off to his friends, "... Erik, wait up dude! Yo Q!"

Ms. Brown stood there rubbing her chin in curiosity.

"Erik?"

CHAPTER 9

They sat outside the band room, Erik was fuming. He wanted to walk off campus but his two friends talked him out of it. Brian was sitting next to him on the bench, patted his shoulder.

"Come on dude, let's go back in."

"Brian, I'm not going back in there. What's the point?"

"The point is that we have to freaking babysit you in case you go into one of your trances again, that's the point! If we're not around then that shadow will take you away then your whole reason for even being here is shot down the toilet." Jordan yelled.

"He's right, Q. You have to be with at least one of us at all times, and neither one of us needs to skip band right now."

Erik stared around. It was hot outside; they were used to this, living in Florida. But Erik still didn't break a sweat.

"Besides dude, you know that if Morgan is right, and as creepy as it seems, she must know what she's talking about, then those things will be back coming for you. They won't stop."

Erik was staring at the ground; his eyebrows were curled in anger.

"Yeah, I know. It just ain't fair, man."

"Yeah, I know. Now come on, let's go back in. AP Brown seems like a bad guy, uh woman, but they do look out for us."

"Are you kidding? They don't really care about us."

"Maybe not all of them, but some of them do man, now come on let's get in the band room."

Brian put his arm around his best friend's shoulder and they got up and walked back to the band room.

When they walked in, the music teacher was already in mid-speech.

"So, with Erik gone, we will be looking for another alto sax to fill in for our trip to Washington DC. Maya has expressed an interest so hopefully, you can get those forms filled in and we can do this. Guys, I was thinking, we can dedicate a song in memory of Erik at the football game this Friday. What do you think?"

"I was going to suggest that, Miss Manley," Maddie said raising her arm.

"Well, I guess it's settled then."

Erik and the guys walked in. The teacher turned to them and placed her hand on her hip.

"Brian Hill, Jordan Lunas why are you guys late?"

Elizabeth was sitting closest to the door and rolled her eyes.

"For someone who's supposed to be under the radar, Erik sure knows how to make an entrance."

Morgan nodded in agreement.

"Uh, sorry Miss Manley, this is my cousin … uh, Marty from California? And he's visiting the school. He may end up going here, or something."

"Oh uh… ok? And you're late because..?"

We were in Miss Brown's office. Brian smiled.

"Ok… get your instruments guys. Marty, you play?"

Everyone in the massive band room turned to him, he glanced around, Morgan and Elizabeth were both shaking their heads 'no'… hoping he'd catch on and know to answer that way.

"Uh… no ma'am, I haven't touched an instrument in… a lifetime."

"Shame, you look like a musician. Anyway, we have MPA's coming up guys. Next Friday is our final football performance then we can concentrate on concert and looking and sounding as good as I know the Wasp Band to be."

Erik sat in the back while everyone got ready to play, within minutes the entire class was deep into a concert piece, and Erik sat in the back, knowing every note the alto saxes were supposed to play. He sat on the chair and closed his eyes. He started to think back to when he was in this room, playing along. He loved playing sax – he had three of them at home.

The song didn't last too long, but before they knew it, Elizabeth was playing her solo when she happened to glance around. Erik wasn't there. She stopped playing and kicked the chair in front of her, it was Kimmy's seat. She turned around, and followed Elizabeth's finger at the empty chair. Then Morgan felt the thump on her chair, she turned around. The look of worry on their faces wasn't something that was easy to hide.

"Oh no!"

Morgan got up, put her flute down on the music stand, and started running for the door. Miss Manley raised her hands and everyone quickly stopped playing.

"Uh Morgan Rubens, do we have a problem?"

"I uh… have to use the bathroom!"

The door slammed behind her as she dashed out scrambling into the hallway.

"Oh, I do too!" Elizabeth screamed.

She handed her clarinet to Isaac who was sitting next to her, then dashed out the door.

Brian and Jordan jumped up, hopping around like they had to go too.

"Oh man, musta been that milk at lunch!" Brian screamed running out.

"No, it was the enchiladas! Yeah, didn't we both eat enchiladas, Brian?" Jordan screamed right behind him.

SLAM!

The sudden shutting of the door caused the schedule on the wall to fall to the floor.

"Really?" the band teacher grimaced.

Christy and Kimmy got up.

"Don't even think about it, you two sit down!" Manley frowned.

Outside, they had made it past the building, Elizabeth and Morgan ran out to the parking lot and looked around. There was no sign of him.

"I'm getting in my car!" Elizabeth said running off.

Jordan and Brian hustled out. Morgan was running for her car on the other side of the student parking lot.

"Brian, come with me! Jordan, go with Elizabeth, hurry!"

The minivan swung around with the side door opened, and Jordan hopped in. Elizabeth went one way and Morgan went the other way, she had just turned the corner on Brandon Boulevard when she saw something that Brian didn't.

"Oh no... that doesn't look good!" she was staring at the Jimmy Johns on the corner, but all Brian saw was the building, cars, and customers.

"Call Elizabeth, tell her to get to Jimmy John's, quick!"

Brian yanked his phone out of his pocket and pressed five... it was Elizabeth's number on speed dial. Morgan punched it and swerved around the corner into the parking lot. She didn't even turn the car off, she wasn't sure how late she was but she had to know. As she hopped out and ran to the door of Jimmy John's, she saw Erik crouched on the other side of the building, he was on his knees and he was covered by a dark cloak. The shadow was there and the agents had Erik covered like a blanket, holding him down against his will. The smile on this being was unnerving to the eye, but luckily, Morgan was the only one who could see it.

"Leave him alone!" she screamed.

"Yeah," Brian yelled in the direction where Morgan was staring, "… leave my best friend alone!"

The being turned to Morgan held out his hand and started squeezing his hand like he was choking someone. To Brian's horror, Morgan also fell to the ground on her knees.

"Morgan!?" Brian jumped down to her, she was holding her throat like she was being robbed of air. He tried, but there was nothing he could do, she was gasping hard and fast.

"Erik! Help her!" he screamed, "… Erik!"

The being floated over to Morgan.

"You are a Reconciler," he grunted under a deep breathy baritone, "… he is mine, you will not interfere. You know the rules, death is my realm, you are but a spectator!"

"I'm not trying to interfere, he just," she choked "… he isn't ready to go!"

"Who isn't ready to go!?" Brian screamed. Morgan was looking up at the being but Brian saw nothing.

"You lie! I have dealt with your kind. You feel your power gives you prestige. Stay away from my claim!"

"No, he just wants to find his killer! Let him find his killer! Brian... I can't... I can't breathe."

"Leave her alone! She isn't doing anything wrong!" he screamed.

The being was well aware of Morgan's powers. She had a certain skill that those in the world of death actually feared, and they could tell a Reconciler a mile away. To the human eye she looked normal, but to a dead person or anyone in the death realm – she emitted a purple aura that stood out. They knew what she could do, and that skill was something they feared, Morgan could send them back to wherever they came from, with a mere touch of her hands. No magic words, no puff of smoke and mirrors, just the touch of her hands. He knew this, he kept his distance.

"You come from a long line of seers, but this is one instance in which you will not prevail."

"I swear to you I am not keeping him here!"

"Then touch him!" he barked.

"He isn't ready to go yet! Don't you understand?" she was on her knees on the ground.

Elizabeth's van screeched to a halt at the scene and some people from the sandwich shop walked out. From their viewpoint, all they saw was Erik curled over on the ground on his knees and Morgan on her knees maybe six feet away from him, holding her throat and screaming at… something. They couldn't see that Erik was physically blanketed by these black invisible cloaks with claws grasping him and holding him down. Brian was leaning down next to Morgan trying to understand, and then Elizabeth and Jordan hopped out of the van and ran to Erik, Brian, and Morgan.

"Touch him!" he barked at the blonde student.

"Morgan, what's going on!?" Elizabeth screamed, "…why are you and Erik on your knees?"

A woman sitting in the restaurant stared out the window, shook her head in disapproval.

"Teenagers." She mumbled

Morgan's choke hold was released and she fell to the hot pavement. Brian rushed and helped her up.

"Touch him or I will take your other friend here." was the command she heard. His bony finger was pointing at Brian. His comment bounced around in her head. She turned to Brian who had no idea what was going on.

"Morgan, are you ok?"

She shook her head.

"No… Brian, I… I have to touch Erik."

"So?"

Elizabeth and Jordan reached her.

"He told me to touch Erik, Brian!"

"Why?"

"Geez you guys don't understand. I'm a Reconciler, if I touch him... he will fade away and his ashes will fall to the floor. That's what we do, that's my... my curse!" she started crying.

"*Who* told you to touch Q? What are you talking about, Morgan!?"

Morgan pointed out. The dark shadow was floating close to Erik, and its annoying laughter bounced around in Morgan's head. No one else could hear or see what she saw.

"Wait... what?" Jordan asked.

"You guys don't understand, what I have is something I wouldn't wish on my worst enemy. My Dad does this for a living, I didn't want these powers, I didn't want them! If I touch Erik, he will die."

"He's already dead!"

"Jordan he will go away! Don't you get it? It's not time for him to go yet, but he... wants him."

"He who? Who is this invisible guy? The devil?" Jordan looked around for even a hint, he saw nothing.

"No... not the devil, death."

Erik was curled over and huffing in pain.

"Get them off me, get them off me, agony, agony..." he kept saying curling his body in affliction.

The agents were all over him, small dark puffs of invisible forms that totally covered him holding him down on the pavement.

"Erik, is your ring still lighting amber?" Morgan called.

"Mmmm, yes." was his painful grunt.

"He isn't ready, this isn't fair." She mumbled to herself.

"Erik, can you get up?" Elizabeth asked.

She walked over and reached for his arm and she felt her hand get slapped away but it wasn't Erik who slapped her hand away, he never moved. She reached out again and once again it was slapped away, but this time she saw a face – and it wasn't a face she'd ever forget.

First it was the teeth, which were more like rotted fangs, but they glistened in the Florida sun. Then she saw the eyes – which were red, bright and concentrating – and shone hard and menacing in her eyes. The actual being was probably two feet tall, but obviously had some kind of strength since it was holding her best friend down on the ground.

"Go…" it said in a low angry mumble.

"Elizabeth, get back in the car." Morgan said.

The being had released Morgan because he knew she had to do what he told her to do. She slowly stood with Brian's help and tears were flowing from her eyes.

"You're not... you're not going to touch him are you, Morgan?" he asked.

"Brian, get in Elizabeth's van." She said wiping her eyes.

"No! You can't do this Morgan!" he yelled.

Brian grabbed her hand and yanked her away from walking toward Erik. He stared her in the eyes, his eyes started to water.

"No! You're not going to do this! I'm not going to let you."

"He commanded; I *have* to Brian."

"No!"

"Brian! I have to do this! *Now get in the van!*" she tore herself away from him.

Brian stood there; Jordan pulled him away. Brian was in tears.

"He's my best friend Morgan... he's my best friend."

She pointed at the van; she didn't even want to look at him. Jordan pulled him away to the van.

"Morgan, please... don't do this." Elizabeth cried.

"Elizabeth, don't make this harder for me, please get in the van. I don't want you guys out here to see what's going to happen."

"Morgan, please..."

Morgan turned away from her and pointed at the van again. Jordan took Elizabeth by the hand, he had his arm around Brian, who was crying, and now pulling Elizabeth away – who was also crying. They went back to her van and she put her head down on the steering wheel and released tears. Jordan stared out at the scene; Morgan was walking up behind Erik.

"Please Morgan," he whispered, "... don't do this."

Morgan looked up; the being was floating there staring back at her awaiting her next move. It had hovered away from Erik but its boney hand kept a steady finger pointed at her friend. Some people in the restaurant had started to walk out, they weren't sure what was going on.

"Erik?" Morgan called in a soft whisper, "... I'm sorry, I have to do this, or there will be no peace. You and I have known each other for a long time and you used to always get on me about being – as you used to call me 'Ms. Goody Two-Shoes'. Well, I know you understand, right?"

Erik didn't say anything, he was just moaning in pain.

"Right, Erik?"

"I don't get it," Jordan said in the van, "... Morgan's known him longer than all of us. They were in elementary school together. We used to call them the twins because they were inseparable in freshman year. How can she do this... this, whatever it is she's going to do to him?"

Her shaking hand got closer.

"I guess this is the only thing to do," Brian said staring out at them, "... if this is a curse she has to live with, man I'm glad I'm not her."

Outside, she was within arms reach of him.

"Erik?"

"Just do it Morgan, get it over with!" he cried in pain, "... just please, get these things off me."

She got closer, Elizabeth's face was down on the steering wheel in despair, but Brian and Jordan were watching, so were all the customers of Jimmy John's, though all they saw was a teenage girl creeping up behind a kneeling, curled over teenaged boy with her hand stretched out.

"I'm... sorry..."

She lowered her hand then pulled out her other hand and both of them quickly jerked down and grabbed Erik on his back.

"Aiiiiiiiiiiiiii!"

The squeal was something everyone there heard. They saw Erik buckle, but then they saw a shadow materialize on Erik's back. It looked like a shadow, but in truth it took the form of a miniature body that became all the more defined as Morgan peeled it off of Erik's back, each of her hands had one of them hanging off her grip as she peeled it off. They were screeching in pain and the sound was unbearable to the ear, it was like a fire truck siren stuck at the highest decibel, mixed with the screeching of tires on a wet road. Everyone close by covered their ears. The beings vanished after seconds of being in her grip, then she reached down and grabbed two more, then two more.

"What are you doing!?" demanded the shadow.

Morgan grabbed the last two, this time everyone watching could see what Morgan saw.

"What the freaking bobbers is that!?" Brian screamed pointing out.

Elizabeth looked up. Morgan was holding the last two in her hands and they became visible. Elizabeth recognized the face, it was what she saw when she tried to touch Erik, then the larger shadow – which was floating there about six feet tall – between Erik and Morgan, suddenly materialized and everyone there saw it in its full glory.

"Oh my God..." the lady sitting in the window gasped, dropping her drink on the floor.

"You cannot do this!" he barked.

Elizabeth sat in shock. The tall shadow slowly took shape and became what looked like a human form under a dark, ripped cloak. The bony hand reached out, pointing at the lone teenager. The two smaller agents in her hand vanished in squeals of pain.

"You have broken the pact! A Reconciler never touches us!" he bellowed in rage.

She turned to him and smiled.

"Bite me!" she screamed, "... Erik run to the van, hurry!"

Erik slowly got up, it was painful, the wig had fallen off, and his make up had smeared. Most of it was wiped off. He turned and faced the van. All witnesses there had a good look at him.

"Go!" Morgan screamed.

The people in the restaurant instantly recognize the dark teenager who was running with a limp toward the open van door. Elizabeth turned it on, revved the engine.

"That... isn't that the kid that got killed last week!?" the woman in the window asked.

A few people had their phones pulled out and had started trying to take pictures and video.

"Hurry!"

Jordan slammed the sliding door and Elizabeth punched it down Kings Avenue. That left Morgan standing alone in a parking lot with a very angry adversary.

"You will perish for this, Morgan Rubens."

"You don't scare me; it isn't my time and you know it."

The witnesses were filming the entire discussion, though on their phones the entity could not be seen. They saw him with their eyes, but the cameras on the phones didn't. On the camera screens it looked like a teenage girl was having an argument, with herself.

"I'm going to get in my car and go to my friends," Morgan smiled, "... and you Sir, can go back to where you came from."

"I am not finished Morgan Rubens! Heed me youthful one, this is not over. I am not finished!"

"Yes... you are."

Morgan got in her car and drove off.

"Nooooo!" the shadow screamed at such a high decibel that several car alarms sounded and some windows burst. He swirled into a tornado-like spin and disappeared. Every witness who was holding out a phone inadvertently dropped their phones because of the thrust of wind and the shock wave that hit them. The sounds of cracking gorilla glass, plastic and metal were the only sounds heard for those few seconds. Then – dead silence.

CHAPTER 10

Elizabeth didn't know where else to go, after miles of aimless driving in and around Brandon, she finally drove home with her friends in the van, including Erik who was exhausted and still moaning. The van sat in the driveway of her home and she was seated there, staring out the window almost as if in shock. No one said anything. Brian turned and Erik was lying on the floor of the van, moaning. Jordan sat in the back seat looking around at all his friends. He'd look down at Erik, then over at Brian who had a blank stare, then at Elizabeth who'd occasionally knock her forehead on her steering wheel – as if in disbelief of everything that had just happened. She turned off the van and let out an exasperated sigh.

The sound of a car door slamming is what broke them all out of their daze. It wasn't a door of *her* vehicle, Elizabeth looked in her rear-view mirror, then her face cringed.

"Oh man, I'm dead."

"Huh?"

"Elizabeth Baker!? What in all that is decent were you thinking? Your music teacher called me, you… you skipped class?! I Had to ask her again and again, 'Are you sure you're talking about my daughter? Elizabeth Baker? My Elizabeth skipped class?'"

Elizabeth turned to her open window. It was her mother and she was in no mood for any kind of excuse.

"Mom…"

"Elizabeth, get out of that car, you are grounded!"

"Mom!?"

She yanked open the door.

"Mrs. Baker…" Brian popped out from behind her.

"Brian Hill, I am so going to tell your mother about this. For you to con my daughter into skipping class…"

"No Mrs. Baker, we didn't con her…" said the other voice in the van.

"Jordan Lunas!? You're mixed up in this too?"

"No, not mixed up... we're involved, see..?"

"Oh you guys are all in so much trouble!"

"It wasn't their fault, Mrs. Baker."

She heard the voice, which was familiar, but she didn't see who it was.

"Oh oh…" Brian quickly hopped out of the van, he knew what was going to happen next. After hanging out with his dead friend, many people who had finally gotten a glimpse of him had one of three reactions; excited to see him, *weirded out* to see him, or fainting.

"Who said that?" Mrs. Baker asked.

She saw the clump of dark hair rise from behind her daughter.

"Uh… I did, Ma'am."

Erik stepped out of the van and faced her.

"Uh... Eri... Eri... ohhh."

She fell into Brian's arms.

"Geez Erik, that was a bonehead move, ya know? What were you thinking?"

"Sorry. Besides I can't think right now, I don't know what those things did to me, but my whole body feels like I've had ants crawling over me, hungry ants, who could smell maple syrup on me, uphill."

"Mom?"

"Hmmm?"

"Mom, are you ok?"

Elizabeth was kneeling next to the sofa in her living room. Her mother was lying there and Brian was fanning her.

"Mom?"

"Oh... Elizabeth, I had the strangest dream, Honey."

She started to get up.

"Uh, Mom, wait..?"

"Hi Mrs. Baker, are you feeling better?"

"Brian?" she sat up. It took a couple of seconds for her eyes to focus across the room, but they did focus and what she saw wasn't necessarily what she wanted to see.

"Hi, Mrs. Baker." Erik stood up and walked toward her.

"I'm dreaming, right? Elizabeth we're in a dream."

She looked at the seriousness on her daughter's face.

"You're going to tell me... I'm not dreaming? Please tell me I'm not dreaming."

"No Mom."

"We can explain, kinda," Erik said kneeling to her.

She stared at him, her eyes followed the contours of his hair, his hands, his face. This was Erik Jason Quince in front of her, but there was something different about him... yet deep inside, she knew...

"Erik, you're dea... no, this isn't happening, how is this happening?"

"I can explain that." came a voice from across the room. It was Morgan. She had arrived while Elizabeth's mom was out cold.

Morgan seemed more troubled than Erik was through all this. She had her reasons, and they'd never understand.

"Erik did die, he really did. But he didn't cross over. He was delayed, I believe he needs to find his killer, then he can truly rest in peace, but until then, he will stay here, unless they come to get him."

"They?"

"Mom. Erik is kinda like... a zombie."

"I'm not a zombie!" he protested smacking his hands on his leg.

"Geez-a. Let it go already!"

"Well, you're still walking among us, Erik. Yet you're dead. Walking... dead... get it?"

"You watch way too much TV, Jordan." Erik shrugged.

"Erik Honey he does make a point," Elizabeth's mother said, "... this is very... awkward."

"You can say that again, Mom."

"In the meantime, we have to figure out how to keep him hidden because a lot of people know him, uh... knew him. Man, you know what I mean." Brian said.

"Yes, I know what you mean, Brian. But this is... this is just not... I don't even know what to call it."

"I'm in limbo until we can do something, like find this jerk," Erik said.

They all stared around at each other then Elizabeth's mother stood.

"Honey, what time is it?" she asked her daughter.

Jordan pulled up his wrist, his watch was dead.

"Hey Erik, can I have your G-Shock watch? The one that lights up? I mean, you won't need it anymore, right?"

"Really Jordan? It's four PM, Mom, why?"

"Well, some of the parents were getting together at Erik's house. His mother asked for a small group to meet, we're going to contribute to an Erik memorial on the spot where he was... where you were, killed. I can't believe this, are you sure I'm not dreaming?"

"No Mom, Erik is really here, and you can't tell anyone. We're still trying to figure it out."

"We have to help him find his killer and this just proved to be a lot harder than we thought it was going to be with those rejects from the Thriller video chasing him." Brian smiled.

"Uh, ok…" she kept staring at Erik in disbelief, "… well the Sheriff is going to be at Erik's house, I'll try and get some answers."

"I'm sorry I got Lizzy in trouble Mrs. Baker; I didn't mean to."

"Oh, forget about that, Erik. How do I explain this to the teacher and keep you all out of trouble? That's my worry now."

"Family emergency?" Brian shrugged.

"Well, we need to get back to my house and hide Erik in the pool house," Jordan told them.

"Absolutely not. Erik, you will stay here in my home." Mrs. Baker said sitting up fully, "… you may sleep in the guest room."

"Uh, I don't sleep, Ma'am."

"Oh, ok."

"That's a good idea though Mom, Morgan can spend the night and we can take turns watching him."

"Watching him?"

"Long story, Mom. You go on ahead to Erik's house, we'll take it from here.

"Ok I'll talk to the parents when I get there, I'm sure your parents were called just as I was about your missing school."

"Mom's already texted me, I'm in trouble." Brian said pouting, "… so I may as well enjoy the rest of today before I get home."

"I'll take care of it." She smiled.

"Thanks, Mrs. Baker."

She got up, still staring at Erik, still trying to grasp the whole thing in her mind. This was against anything she'd ever believed. Jordan walked up to Erik and started pressing buttons on his watch. Erik yanked his hand away.

"You're not getting my watch, dude."

The ring on his finger was shining the bright amber light but it wasn't as intense as before.

"I'm going to go home and get some clothes and stuff, and we need to put make-up on Erik again for tomorrow," Morgan said.

She stared at Erik's ring for a few seconds.

"Yeah, may as well drop us off then." Brian got up and followed her. She stood close to Erik.

"We'll get through this, Erik." She motioned to touch him, then stopped her hand midway, "... sorry, I have to keep catching myself and remember not to touch you."

"Yeah, not a good idea." Brian smiled.

"She can't help it, it's human nature," Jordan smirked.

"I'll text Kimmy and ask her to come over, she lives down the block, and we can have a makeup session with Erik tonight," Elizabeth told them.

"Geez, what is this, a slumber party?" he whined.

"Oh, snap guys! Look!"

Jordan was pointing at the TV that was on and he grabbed the remote and raised the volume. They were viewing a replay of the scene they had just left less than an hour ago at the Jimmy John's parking lot.

"...This is footage from a viewer's phone. In it you can clearly see what resembles the fallen teenager from last week. Is it a twin? An imposter? What exactly were these kids doing out of school and staging this scene out at a Brandon restaurant? The viewing public has a right to know and we will have updates as they come in. Now back to our scheduled program."

"Wow, we made the news! It's true what they say," Jordan smiled, "... I looked ten pounds heavier on the screen."

"Dude will you get serious!? They just showed Erik on TV and they showed us and Morgan!" Brian said.

"So?"

"So now we really have to keep him in hiding."

"Where are we going to keep him, Morgan? They'll find out each of our names and camp out in front of our houses." Elizabeth told her.

"We've gotta put him somewhere."

"He's staying right here in my home, I dare a newsman to try and get in my house." Mrs. Baker said.

"Man, I love how you guys all talk about me like I'm dead or something."

"Erik, shut up!" Morgan sighed.

"Ok well, we have to really plan this out. We can't let them know that what they saw on the news was actually true," Elizabeth said, "... we need to split up and regroup tomorrow."

"Come on guys," Morgan walked toward the door, "... I'll take you two home."

"Wait, Morgan, can I ask you something?"

"Sure, Erik."

"I notice you keep staring at and asking me about my ring, what gives?"

Morgan stared at him then around at the others in the room. She was with-holding something and Erik has known her too long for her to hide it.

"It's nothing, Erik. Come on, guys."

"No, Morgan. Really. You told me I couldn't take it off and it's true, I can't. What's the deal with this ring and this weird glow?"

"Yeah aside from the fact that it acts like a radar to that creep out there trying to get him. You told us about it, but there's more, isn't there?" Brian asked.

Morgan stepped closer to Erik, they were almost eye to eye but would not touch each other.

"Erik, if that light dims and starts to turn red, then you have only hours before it ends up falling off your finger. Then you're his for good. Right now, he has to fight you to bring you back, once the color changes, you won't be able to resist him at all. I doubt that there's anything I could do either, we probably won't even be able to help you at all."

"So, either way, he's dead anyway, right? I mean, ok ok... he's dead already I know, but I mean, if the ring turns red, then he'll just like vanish or something?" Jordan asked.

"Pretty much." She shrugged.

"Screw that! I can't go till I get this guy and you guys know this, he's running around free and I'm a monster because of him, well I'm not going down like that, this is a fight to the end."

"Yeah we know, Buddy. And we're going to get him – *the Quatro* is on the case... well, quatro plus one." Brian smirked pointing at Morgan.

"Uh, yeah. Come on guys, I'll take you home." Morgan said.

They followed her to the car. It was afternoon but it felt like it was later and Elizabeth sent a quick text out to Kimmy on her phone. Erik walked up to his friend, Elizabeth – his rock. The leader of *the Quatro* and for the first time since all this has started, he actually felt helpless. They stared into each other's eyes.

"Erik, we'll get through this."

"Don't really matter; think about it, either way, I'm dead."

"You're already dead."

"Duh, I mean. If we find this guy and get him turned in or whatever, or the ring turns red... either way, in the end, I won't be a part of you guys anymore. Lizzy, it's really over."

"Don't talk like that Erik."

"But don't you see? It's true. This ain't fair, I didn't ask for this."

"Then why did you have to try and play hero and try to stop those guys? Why didn't you just let them run with the money?"

"Because it's wrong."

"Who cares!? That's a job for the police, not a high school senior!" she stomped her foot on the floor when she said that.

"I couldn't just stand there and do nothing, Lizzy! It's just like Johnny in school, if you keep letting him get away with it, he'll have free reign. Well not on my watch!"

"So, you chose to be a hero!? That's great, that's just freaking great Erik! You being a Good Samaritan got you killed!" she slammed her hand on the back of the couch in a rage-filled swing.

Erik looked in her eyes, they were getting watery. She was so sad, but she was full of anger too.

"I'm sorry Lizzy, I know. You're right. Nothing I can do about it now."

"It's not fair Erik, we were all supposed to go to college together and grow old together and walk in each other's weddings and stuff. You're supposed to be my first child's Godfather. I was going to babysit your kids... it's, ruined. You're my best friend Erik, I feel all alone now." She started crying.

He lowered his head, and turned away.

"You are not alone; I am here with you…"

They walked away from each other to different sides of the room.

"You know, right now I need you guys. And this isn't just for me, those guys can hurt other people. We need to come together…"

She turned and stared out the window. The serene Brandon night was quickly coming. It would be dark in a couple of hours. Though it was fall, the humidity in the air was common for Florida.

Morgan backed her Jeep Liberty out of the grass and drove off, unaware that Elizabeth was standing at the window, watching. The view of the street from the lone tree in Elizabeth's yard was like one off a movie set of a quiet neighborhood getting ready for a beautiful Florida sunset. The sun hadn't even begun to set, but there was already a shadow in the tree, a shadow with red fiery eyes that followed the trail of the SUV as it drove off.

Elizabeth sat with Erik in the den, he picked up the remote and turned on the TV.

"I miss TV," he mumbled.

"Erik what are we going to do? That thing is going to keep coming after you till it gets you. I saw it, he means business. He's not going to stop, you know? What are we going to do?"

"I don't know Lizzy."

"And what was it you did to Johnny that made him fall back like he did in the hallway? You barely touched him. That was weird. Ha, you scared the fart out of him!"

"I don't know…"

"And how does Morgan have this weird power? I've never heard of a Reconciler…"

"Lizzy I don't know, I don't know!"

She turned to him after watching the Jeep finally turn the corner out of her neighborhood.

"Man for a dead person, you sure are clueless."

"I know." He smiled.

They both started laughing.

Morgan drove down Kingsway Avenue with her two friends in the car. Jordan was in the passenger seat and was staring at her. Brian sat in the back seat staring out the window. The Jeep turned and headed east, Morgan was deep in thought herself but couldn't stop but feeling that she was being watched, stared at, followed. She could feel the burning eyes on her. She turned and Jordan was glaring at her.

"*What,* Jordan?!"

"I, I uh… Morgan, it's just kinda creepy, you know? I've known you for four years since we started going to Victoria, I would have never figured you to be a medium."

"I'm not a medium, I don't believe in that stuff."

140

"Ha! You don't believe in that stuff? Morgan, have you ever wondered how we all felt before we found out about you? I sure didn't believe in... in whatever it is you are till I saw it with my own eyes. I sure as heck believe now!"

"Well mediums are different; a lot of them usually are scam artists. I don't scam people, I don't even tell people about me, this just kinda happened with you guys finding out, no one's supposed to know. Erik's known about it since we were in fifth grade."

"Why did you tell him?"

"I didn't, he kinda had to find out the hard way."

"The hard way? Why? What happened?"

Brian turned and paid attention too from behind her. Morgan seemed visibly uneasy about sharing the story, but she figured that maybe if she told them, they'd understand her a little better. Their curiosity bothered her, but curiosity was a part of who these two were, they were always asking questions and it annoyed her. She turned on Clay Avenue.

"When I was in fifth grade, Mom and Dad took me and Erik to Ybor City. There's this ghost tour, they walk you through different parts of the Historic sections and they tell you stories and you see things that... well you see things that are cool and interesting, but I saw things that I shouldn't have seen."

Her mind went into like a haze, it was a flashback about to happen and she tried not to remember, but this time… she had to – for her friends, she had to remember the time.

"I grew up in Orlando, then we moved here when I was in fourth grade. Dad used to get calls from all kinds of people for paranormal stuff. When I was five, I saw my first ghost. There was this white cloudy face that used to follow me around my house. Sometimes I would talk to it. I would get mad because it never said anything; it just followed me around the house. So, one day I asked it to stop following me, it would just look at me and smile. It was like a face in a small cloud, and it was always right at my face level and would float about three feet away from me.

I would tell Mom about it and she said I had a great imagination. Mom always had a hard time accepting all this stuff. Then one day I came home from school and I was mad because this girl stole my Power Puff girls backpack, and I ran to my room and I was crying and the cloudy face floated next to me and I looked up and it was smiling and it made me more mad. I reached out and grabbed it and the look on it's face went from happy to pain and then it made this choking sound, then it vanished. And I never saw it again. I told my dad about it that night and that was when he sat me down and explained it all to me, he told me that I had 'the gift'. I call it 'the curse'.

Then in fifth grade we went on that ghost tour. The lady kept saying stuff like "if you look over there, you might see the ghost of a lady named Prudence Fipwhistle." I looked up and I said, "She isn't there, she's over there." And I pointed right at her.

The tour guide laughed it off, but then the ghost pushed a lamp off the table. Obviously she didn't like that I saw her. The tour guide said she'd never seen anything like that on a tour. And I told her that the ghost was real and she was standing right next to her. She laughed again and then her hair got pushed back and forth by Miss Fipwhistle. She didn't like people not believing that she was really there. I started talking to her and then the tour lady said I was some kind of possessed freak, then Mommy slapped her and I wanted to go home. Miss Fipwhistle wanted me to stay but Dad told her that we had to leave and then another ghost came out of the wall and started arguing with my Dad and I got mad and I ran over and I screamed at him to leave my dad alone... and I..."

They got to a red light and the car stopped.

"You what, Morgan?"

"I... touched him..."

She lowered her head, almost as if in shame.

"And?" Brian asked.

"And a bright light happened, he turned to ashes and the ashes fell from my hands to the ground, everyone there saw it, and everyone there ran. I can still remember the look on Erik's face."

She drove out into the intersection of Sydney and Valrico Road. She was still talking and didn't notice the car speeding towards her from the left. It would prove too late when the last thing she heard was the hard screeching of tires.

The sound of contact was cruel to the ears. She heard Brian scream "Oh my freaking bobbers!"

Then she blacked out after the second tumble of the car on Wheeler Road. Outside, at a distance but still within view, a dark shadow perched above an electric pole shone an evil proud grin, displaying its half skull and rotted teeth. He looked down at the crash. The Jeep was upside down in a ditch and the car that hit it had also rolled over sideways and was resting against the gas pump of the lone gas station.

"4,3,2,1..." the shadow counted on it's bony fingers.

KA-*BLOOM*!

The gas pump exploded sending the car back in the air and headed straight to Morgan's upside-down Jeep.

"Morgan, are you o..."

The sudden jolt of the weight of the car against the Jeep shoved it deeper into the damp ditch.

"That's what I wanted to see..." the shadow smiled.

It smacked it's hands together, as if congratulating itself, then floated off into the sky.

"Morgan!"

Erik hopped up on the couch at Elizabeth's house as if waking from a horrible nightmare. He ran for the door and hoofed it out into the street.

"Erik? Wait, what are you..? Erik!"

Elizabeth ran out after him. Their friend Kimmy was just walking up the drive.

"Kimmy, get in the van, let's go!"

"Uh... ok?"

"Morgan?"

It was faint, she heard her name but she also was overwhelmed by a bright warm light, the tighter she closed her eyes... the brighter it got. It was warm on the skin, almost like sunlight but it didn't burn, no, actually it was very soothing. Then the next thing that caught her senses was the smell, fresh flowers, or something. It was sweet, radiant, and surrounded her.

"Morgan?"

The voice, it was Brian. And he sounded like he was in pain.

"Morgan? I think I'm going to die."

She looked around, though she felt totally consumed in the light, there was a dark splotch right in front of her and a hand was reaching into the light from it.

"Morgan?"

"Brian, are you ok?"

"I... I don't know. I can't feel anything. Jordan... are you here?"

They didn't hear Jordan at all.

"Jordan?"

Morgan looked around; she glanced up and down, looking for a sign. She'd lost her sense of direction because no matter where you looked, whether it was up, down left right, behind you – it was just bright light. She couldn't be dead, it wasn't her time. She knew... Morgan Rubens felt she was immune to death because of her... condition, or as she called it, her curse. She'd felt that way all her life.

"Ok guys, listen to me. Brian, Jordan, you're both very close by to each other. We were in an accident, we can't separate, do you hear me? We can't separate." she said with authority.

"Oh God... oh God... it's one of those things!" Brian screamed.

"What things!?" She could hear him but she couldn't see him.

"Those things that were covering Erik in the parking lot... he's coming for me Morgan!"

"Stretch out your hand Brian! Let me try and feel for you! Hurry!"

She could see nothing but bright light no matter where she looked, all except for the one splotch of darkness about the size of a basketball, about three feet away from her. It radiated in the air like it was frozen there, tempting her to touch it.

Outside, the gas station attendant called 911 and ran out to the cars. The one on top had caught flame and Morgan's car would too in only a matter of time. From where the man stood, he could see Morgan, Brian and Jordan in the car – still in their seat belts, in the ditch and they weren't moving. The driver of the other car started screaming and was pounding on his door.

"Help! Help me!!"

The gas station attendant took a chance and hopped on Morgan's upside-down car and carefully climbed to the one on top of it. He could see the man through the window and he yanked on the door.

"Help me!' screamed the man.

"Are you ok? You're not supposed to move anyone in an accident!" he said.

"Screw that man, my car's going to explode, pull me outta here!"

The man took hold of his arm, and then slowly pulled him out of the car.

"Are you in pain, my friend?" he asked holding on to him.

"Hurry... the car's going to blow. Come on!"

They managed to climb down and he help the man away from the wreckage and put him to rest against the building. He then turned back to the toppled cars again. The three friends were motionless in the Jeep underneath. He saw no movement of any kind.

"Hurry Brian, see if you can find Jordan! We don't have a lot of time!"

"I don't see him, Morgan! Oh God, Oh God, we're going to die!"

"Reach for my hand, come on!"

"Is your hand out?"

"Yes, right here... I can hear you, so you have to be close by. Grab my hand!"

He saw a hand poke out from the light and he quickly grabbed it. Something inside her told her to avoid the hand in the dark hole and she did.

"Is that you, Morgan?"

"Yes... reach out your other hand, try and grab for Jordan he has to be close to you. Hurry!"

"I'm trying! I'm trying!"

Brian turned around, in the blinding light, he saw another hand reach out for his, right behind him. It had a ring on, a ring with a bright amber glowing jewel. It reached in, grabbed Brian by the sleeve and yanked him out. Brian held on to Morgan, both friends were pulled from the wreckage and carried to the trees across the street where they lay slightly breathing. Brian felt pain, he felt heat, but then he felt someone brush his hair back. He lazily opened his eyes.

"Am, am I dead?"

"No Brian."

He looked up at the hand with the ring, then followed the arm with his eyes up to the person's face.

"Erik?"

"Yeah buddy."

"Morgan, are you alright?"

It was Jordan's voice, just to the right of him. She heard the sirens approaching in the distance, but she didn't move.

"Morgan?"

Brian sat up, Jordan was crouched over on his knees trying to revive Morgan, she didn't move. He was holding on to his arm, it looked like he was in pain.

"Morgan?"

He budged her, she didn't respond. Erik walked up to her but made sure not to touch her.

"Morgan!?"

She only slightly heard their voices, it came in and out, faded, reverberated. But she was still having visions of the black hole inside before they got pulled out. She was still seeing visions of the hand that was poking through the black hole, the hand that kept taunting her to grab at it. A hand that almost looked like Brian's but couldn't have been because his voice was coming from just behind her to the left and the black hole with the hand was just in front of her slightly to the right.

Morgan Rubens wasn't happy with her curse, but for once her instinct caused her to do the right thing as far as she was concerned. That hand could only have been one thing… the hand of death.

The screeching tires close by made them turn to the sound, the van looked familiar, it could only be one person, Elizabeth. Kimmy hopped out right behind her in a rush.

"Erik! Why did you run off like a banshee out of… Oh… oh no! What happened to Morgan's car!?"

She ran up to them; saw Morgan lying on the grass. She and Kimmy bent down to her.

"Morgan? Can you hear me!?"

"Don't touch her Lizzy!" Erik barked.

The ambulance rushed up, the blinding red lights illuminated the corner of Valrico Road and Sydney along with the fire just across the street at the gas station. The fire truck hurried to the scene and the firemen quickly worked on quenching the flames, but just across the street the group of high school students had other worries.

"My friend, she's hurt!" Elizabeth cried out.

"You have to revive her, we can't let her get away." Brian gasped to the paramedic.

"Let her get away?"

"Go away, get dead, croak, kick the bucket... whatever! Just don't let my friend Morgan die!"

The EMT rushed over to her. Erik's ring started glowing again. He backed off and walked into the woods, he didn't want too many people to see him. This was no accident, he knew deep inside that this was deliberate. Now he was dealing with supernatural forces and he had no idea how to combat it, but he was sure going to give it his best. Sure, he was dead, but Morgan going through this was just not fair. He turned and started to walk away.

"Erik?" Jordan called. He reached out and his arm shot a painful spurt so bad that his whole body jerked to the reaction.

"Ow!" he screamed.

"Jordan?" Elizabeth ran to his side.

"My arm, Elizabeth, I think it's broken!"

That made Erik fume even more. This wasn't their fight, it was his. Why did he – whoever he – the agent of death was – have to involve his friends?

"You guys stick with Morgan, I have to find somebody, there's going to be a fight tonight." He turned and ran off into the woods.

"Q!?" Brian called.

Kimmy stood, watched them put Morgan on the gurney.

"Brian, grab her phone – we need to call her Mom."

"Man, we are not going to be popular with parents in Brandon, Florida. We're going to be the hated ones." Jordan sighed.

Brian handed Elizabeth the phone and she walked off into the street searching the contacts on Morgan's phone.

Brian and Jordan felt a little pain, Jordan more than Brian. And they weren't sure if they'd need treatment there or have to be taken to the hospital. Kimmy followed the carrier with Morgan to the back of the ambulance.

"Morgan? Can you hear me? We're calling your Mom... Morgan?"

Nothing.

Elizabeth connected with Morgan's mother, and she burst into tears. So much so that Kimmy had to take the phone and explain it all. Elizabeth went back over to Jordan and Brian who were both sitting up on the grass. Jordan was getting a splint on his arm. Elizabeth was crying and Brian held her there on the grass.

"It's ok Elizabeth, Erik's going to fix this. I really feel like he... he's going to fix this."

"I know Brian," she sniffed, "... but you know... all this stuff happening is his fault because he refused to die. And when you guys go through stuff I go through stuff, we're *the Quatro,* I feel like you guys are all just another part of me."

"We all feel that way Elizabeth," Jordan said, "... ow!" the paramedic had just snapped the flint into place, it caused Jordan to jump in pain.

"Well, he's out there... Erik's out there, and he's going to start all out war now."

"Excuse me, aren't you kids... weren't you on the news, that video?" one of those tending to them asked.

"Uh..."

Jordan was going to say yes but Elizabeth's stern stare told him not to.

"Uh... what video?" he smiled.

"That kid that walked off, that was the dead kid, wasn't it?"

The three friends just stared around at each other and said nothing.

In back of the ambulance, Morgan lay still, quiet barely breathing.

"Stop fighting me, cross over Reconciler. Cross over."

She heard the voice, the deep gravel voice of her enemy. It bounced around in her head. She could sense herself walking down a hallway, a dark hallway like in school, maybe the school library, dark shelves on either side of her, and there was a bright light just ahead. She could hear someone walking; they were going to walk across that spot where she was headed.

"Erik?"

She stopped and stared down the short corridor. The light was blinding, but whoever was walking was doing so at a slow pace and they were going to cross paths in a matter of seconds. She covered the top of her eyes to help shade from the light and started slowly walking up toward the light again. Then just ten feet away from the opening where the bookshelves ended and the light sat, she saw a form walking by.

"Erik?"

It was a shadow of an image, it stopped, turned, and stared right at her with red concentrating eyes. Then a slow smile.

"You are in *my* world now, Reconciler!" he smiled.

She turned and started running away and he chased her down the long seemingly endless corridor of empty bookshelves.

Back on the gurney in back of the ambulance, Kimmy was standing at the still open door and had just hung up with Mrs. Rubens, Morgan's mother.

"Morgan, I just spoke to your mom, she's going to meet us at the hospital. I hope you hear me Morgan, I'm not going to leave your side, I'll be there."

The paramedic slammed the door and unseen to Kimmy or the EMT, a slow single tear dripped from Morgan's eye.

CHAPTER 11

Night had seemed to creep early and fast this evening. Brian and Jordan were both also taken to the Emergency Room, but they were ok, considering the dilemma they had just endured. Brian got out with just a sprain but Jordan had to wear a sling on his arm.

Brian was home now; he sat alone in his room. In the span of a week, life as he knew it had changed dramatically, his best friend was killed and now another close friend lay in what seemed like a coma at the Brandon Regional Hospital. This was more grief than he had encountered his whole life.

Kimmy was allowed to ride with Morgan on the ambulance. Elizabeth drove to Christy's house and picked her up. Her destination - Erik's house, she knew there was a get together of parents and she wanted to be a part of it. Since Erik's death she'd been shunned by his parents and she was once very close to them. The plan was to attend the memorial meeting, then right after she was going back to the hospital to see Morgan. Christy was filled in on everything that had happened and she sat there in disbelief.

"Why is all this stuff happening?" she asked.

Elizabeth had no answer. She was tired, her dark brown hair was up in a semi ponytail and she was hoping that the meeting hadn't finished.

They got out of the van and approached the door.

"I don't have a good feeling about this, Elizabeth."

Elizabeth turned to her and nodded, signaling that she felt the same way, then she swallowed, and softy knocked on the door.

"Elizabeth, can I go see Morgan with you after this?" Christy asked.

"Sure, I just want to…"

"What are you doing here!?"

The scream jolted both of them. They turned to the door and Erik's Mom was standing there, glaring through the screen.

"Uh, Hi Mrs. Quince, we wanted to come to the meeting and see if we could…"

"You are not welcomed here in my house, Elizabeth!"

Elizabeth's Mom came running up behind Erik's mom and was followed by Erik's dad.

"Go!" she screamed at the teenager. The look on her face gave it away, she had been crying probably for hours, and rage had set in.

"Mrs. Quince, please… I just want to…"

"I said go!" she pointed out to the front yard, "… my baby would be here right now if it weren't for you, leave my house!"

"Honey, wait now," her husband comforted behind her, "… Elizabeth was one of his best friends."

"I don't care!"

Several other mothers came and held her, she was trembling in what seemed a mixture of rage and a nervous breakdown that was sure to come. Gail Quince was at her wit's end and seeing Elizabeth didn't help.

"Elizabeth Honey," her mother smiled, "… maybe you should go. I'll talk to her."

"But Mom..?"

"Sweety, please."

Erik's dad walked out, put his arms around both girls and walked them back to the van.

"Guys, I'm sorry you had to go through that. It's going to take my wife some time to uh… accept all this. She is broken, I don't even know what to do but to be there for her. My son… our, son, was…" he choked up.

"I'm so sorry Mr. Quince, we're all hurting over this, you know?"

"You can call me David."

"Ok, Mr. David, uh… I wish she knew how bad we hurt with Erik gone too. I know he was your son but he was our friend." Christy said.

"He was my best friend. There's a hole in our lives now with him gone and none of us are going to get over it." Elizabeth added.

"Elizabeth, just give her some time. She's always liked you, just give her some time."

"Thanks Mr. uh... David." Christy smiled.

Inside the house, Gail Quince was in the middle of a crying fit that no one there could console.

"Mi nene, mi nene precioso. Hay Dios mio, mataron a mi nene!"

Most of the people in the house didn't understand her cries in her native tongue for her son, but they understood the pain. Outside, Elizabeth was backing out and she drove off into the night. David Quince slowly walked back in, passing the massive water oak tree in the front yard. Just years ago, he and a very young Erik hung a swing off the huge limb above him. He held onto the rope, composed himself.

"Come on Dave… be strong. She needs you to be strong." Then he looked up at the rope as it looped over the branch and remembered young Erik excitedly climbing the tree to loop it. He was so proud of himself and David remembered that Saturday morning.

"Who needs Spiderman when I have Spider-Erik to the rescue?" he smiled. Erik laughed. David reminisced on that day, now staring up the dark tree. Then tears started.

"I miss you son… miss you bad."

"David, are you still out there?" called Elizabeth's mom, "… we're picking the design now."

He wiped his eyes with his shirt.

"Coming."

He didn't see the shadow on the other side of the tree. He walked to the screen door and pulled it open, exhaled and walked into the house.

Back at the tree, just on the other side to where he was standing, a head popped out and stared at the house. The dark clump of curly hair was unmistakable, had David stayed outside a few more minutes, he might have seen him. But remaining hidden was the prime directive for him, Erik had to stay hidden from his own parents, knowing the anguish they were going through. It didn't really hit him till now, no longer would he be able to stay up late in his room playing X-Box games, or watching old movies on TCM, or chatting with the Quatro online for hours. His fish Jack would be alone, his dog Rogue wouldn't have someone to play with afterschool anymore. And his Mom and Dad wouldn't have someone to make popcorn on family movie nights. His parents, now that his big sister had moved out – would be alone. After he saw and heard the breakdown his mother just had with just the presence of Elizabeth, he knew their lives would never be the same. And for the first time, he saw his father cry.

"Dad…" he breathed, "… I miss you too."

Then he thought about Morgan. She was in a coma and lying on a hospital bed. Now her parents will go through what his parents are enduring right now, and all this because he refused to die. His sadness turned into a frown. He turned and walked away out into the darkness.

In the hospital room, Morgan's mother was sitting by the bed and staring at her daughter. Morgan had a breathing tube and didn't move. A tear slowly dripped down her mother's cheek. Cathy Rubens was used to weird things happening in her daughter's life. She detested the gift her daughter was given but understood that it was a normal part of her life – normal being a questionable word. Nothing was ever normal in the Rubens household. Even a visit to the local Publix could turn into an adventure. Cathy knew about her husband's gift early on, but she was sure that her youngest daughter would be... normal. After all, her oldest daughter who now lived in New Orleans was. She thought back on it, she should have caught it when, as a little girl, Morgan always talked about her invisible friend Giselle.

"That should have been my sign." She sighed.

Then she heard someone at the door.

"Mrs. Rubens?"

She turned, two fellow students walked in, both band members at school and both close to Morgan.

"Oh...Maddie, Maya, hi."

"How is she doing?"

"We don't really know. She hasn't moved since she got here."

"I thought Kimmy was here, she texted us." Maya smiled.

"She got picked up by her Dad."

Maddie walked over and hugged her, Maya went over to the bed and touched Morgan's hand.

"I'm so sorry, Mrs. Rubens. First Erik, now this... I just don't believe it. It's like there's a curse on Victoria High or something." Maya sighed.

"Morgan's strong, she will get through this." Maddie smiled.

"How's your husband taking this?"

"He's on his way from some town called Danica."

Maddie knew the family, she'd spent time at Morgan's house before and even babysat the dogs when they went on vacation. Maya was strictly a school/band friend but the three of them sat at lunch together a lot.

"She's going to pull through this, Mrs. Rubens." Maya smiled.

They all smiled at each other, then slowly rested their eyes back on Morgan.

Just outside the window, a familiar vengeful shadow stood. It's bony hands rested on the windowsill and it's concentrating red fiery eyes stared at the four in the room. They didn't know it, but he was communicating with Morgan as she lay there motionless.

"Give in to me." he muttered in his head to her. He knew she could feel him. Though she made no physical movement and the scanners showed very slow brain activity, Morgan was still running down the long dark bookshelf hallway. And he was close on her tail.

"Give in to me Reconciler!"

"No! Leave me alone!"

"Death is imminent, can you feel it?" he laughed.

His laughter bounced around in her head and it was torture, yet to her mother and two friends surrounding her – they saw no movement.

At the Lunas home, Jordan sat in his room with the TV on. He had his left arm in a sling and was lying back on his bed staring at the ceiling. Flashbacks of the accident replayed in his mind. His mom rushed to the hospital to get him and by the time she got there he was ready to be released, though they had him heavily sedated. She got him in the car and rushed home, not knowing that Morgan was just three rooms down. He rubbed his fingers across the remote, not even paying attention to what was on the thirty-seven-inch flat screen attached to his wall.

"Erik, where are you, man? *The Quatro* is falling apart."

He picked up the remote and started flipping channels, he stopped after he saw a familiar face on the screen, then he raised the volume.

"... young Erik Quince was struck down way too early in his life. For over a week, his killer has been at large, but police believe they have the man in custody now. Here is footage from just minutes ago from a viewer's cell phone over at the Falkenburg Road jail. The suspect, thirty-year-old Daniel S. Keith, is a known felon with a hefty criminal record. Robbery, battery, arson, this man has had no business being on the streets yet was released each time on a technicality."

Jordan sat up, grabbed his phone and dialed.

"... a reporter is headed toward the building as we speak and see if we can get a statement from the Hillsborough County Sheriff's Department. Stay tuned for more details at eleven."

"Erik *so* has to hear about this!"

BEEP BREEP!

The cell phone went off and startled her. Elizabeth was still driving but Christy took her phone, looked at the number.

"It's Jordan."

"Answer it."

"Yo, what's up Jordan?"

"Christy? They have the guy that killed Erik! He's at the jail right now!"

"What!?"

BREEP BREEP!

He picked up the phone, he was lying in his room in the dark and placed the iPhone to his ear.

"Yeah? Wait a minute, *What!?*"

Brian turned on his TV, switched to News Channel 8. His jaw dropped at the sight on the screen. Isaac, one of the guys from band in school, called to tell him of the latest news that was catching fire all over Brandon. He had just hit 'end' to hang up when his phone went off again, he hit send.

"Christy? Yeah man, I just heard! So you guys are coming over? Cool, I'll be outside!"

He put his phone on the bed and got up to put his new Nike's on.

"Man, I sure wish Erik was here! This is the moment he's been waiting for and we have no way to get in touch with him! Where is Q?"

Erik stood alone in the woods just outside the Brandon Regional Hospital. The small pond close by reflected the moonlight off just enough to give light to his dark surroundings.

"Where are you!?" he screamed.

Erik looked around in quick jerks of his head. He knew that the entity was close by, he could feel him, but he wouldn't make himself known. That fried Erik.

"Come on! You've been chasing me since I got back! What, are you afraid to face me now!? Come on!" he stomped his foot on the ground in rage.

Suddenly there was a quick rustle in the bushes behind him, he glanced around. The bush moved but nothing was there.

"You have to play games? Come on, you want me, I'm here!"

He heard another sound just behind him, sounded like a child's giggle. He turned around and saw the red eyes of one of the diminutive Agents of Death crawl out from behind the bush, then another one next to him, then another one in front of him. Their smile was unnerving. They stood about two feet tall, were basically a shadow that was almost in the shape of a big bat with short legs, red eyes, short tight fangs and three fingered claws for hands. Their faces were what was the most gruesome about them. The red glowing eyes were set apart wide, and the contour of a nose was there but there was no nose, and their mouths took up most of the space of the face. A smile went from ear to creepy ear and fangs lined up in a neat row. They mumbled to themselves. Another one dropped from the tree to the right of Erik and slowly walked over to him, started sniffing him.

He stood there, tightened his fists, fury was all they saw in his dark eyes.

"Come on, come on you little spineless creeps, you wanna fight? You had to come here because your boss man is a coward? I ain't scared of you!" he barked.

"Nor do they fear you, young Quince."

It was a deep baritone voice that came from nowhere right in front of him. Erik heard the voice, but then he felt the fierce slap across his face. The force sent Erik to the ground in a bone shattering thud. But he got back up.

"Funny you call me a coward. I do not cower, I cannot cower... you see, I am death. All of mankind cowers from me. It's silly when you think about it, you are born, you live, you will die. It's the only one certain thing in life that every human knows. You will die."

Erik turned to the voice, he still couldn't see him.

"You forget, Jerk – I'm already dead. You failed."

Erik heard the quick sound of a hand moving through the air.

SMACK!!

Again, another fierce slap across his face that sent him back against a tree. The smaller ones were giggling, they all huddled around him and chuckled together.

"That the best you got?" Erik wiped his cheek pulling himself off the tree.

"Such bravery from someone on the verge of losing his very soul. My suggestion to you, young man, is that you close your eyes and hope that this is just imagination."

Erik saw the eyes materialize first, right in front of him. Then the form of the head, dark – like a shadow - appeared. Then the cloak which draped his whole body slowly took shape. He wasn't standing, he floated, he never touched the ground.

"I see you no longer answer the call. That can only mean one thing."

"What call? What are you talking about?!" Erik stood firm and faced him, planting his heels firmly in the ground. Erik was ready for a fight.

The agents surrounded him, they stood as if awaiting a command. Erik quickly raised his right foot, and with the accuracy of a pro connected his size nine Converse against the being's face. It did connect and sent him back against the tree. But he bounced back off the tree in a split second and with dead aim grabbed Erik by the throat.

"Erik Quince, you belong to me. You cheated me and I don't take to cheaters lightly. This is not an incident I will let go – you belong to me. This isn't a pitiful brawl in the halls of some puny high school, this is fate – you can't win."

"Dude, you need Listerine."

"You jest, I was told you were ever the joker. Yet you see Quince, the joke is now on you."

He lifted Erik in his strong grip then shoved him away. He landed on his back on the grass. The agents quickly surrounded him.

"I have the power to have them attack you and rip you apart. It would be delightful to watch. You have been nothing but a nuisance to me."

"You could have taken me a long time ago punk, what is it that keeps you from doing that, this ring?"

Erik pulled out his hand to show him.

"Ah, the Parting Stone. Have you not noticed, Quince that the glow has since faded?"

"Huh?"

Erik looked at the stone, it wasn't amber anymore, it was starting to glow a dim red. He remembered what Morgan had told him, he looked at it again.

"Wait... what?"

"Yes, soon the ring will be of no use to you. The beacon in the ring draws me to you. The beacon has linked us. You are soon ready to depart this earth, but I have a proposition."

"Ha! *You* have a proposition... are you kidding?"

Erik slowly got up.

"You and your proposition can bite me where the sun doesn't shine, Junior!"

"Ah, ever the rebel, you will have to learn just where you stand, Quince. I am the victor."

"Victor? I don't give a crap what your name is!"

The shadow floated back, then pointed at him.

"I tire of your charades. Get him!" he barked.

The agents had no issue following orders, they attacked en masse and within seconds had covered Erik in a black cloak that rendered him back painfully down to his knees. It felt like a million bees stinging at the same time, and along with the stinging came a high pitch noise that resonated in his head and only got higher as the seconds passed. It was like the sound from an alarm clock and the off switch was broken, and he couldn't shake it off no matter what he did. Between the constant chomping and humming sounds from these horrid minions, he was in unbearable agony.

"No, stop... please! Get them off me! Get them off me!!"

The agent's fangs were chopping fast and hard, though they didn't leave any trace of tooth marks or blood of any kind, Erik felt like they were killing him. If he swatted one off, it came back within seconds and stayed on the same spot.

"Please!? Make them stop!"

"You will consider my proposition, then young Quince?" he laughed.

"Yes, *YES!* Anything! Just get them off me!"

The shadow raised his boney palm and one by one the agents dispersed off into the trees until the two were the only ones left standing in the woods.

Erik was on his knees on the ground, panting heavily, drained, and rubbing his entire body of the annoying stinging sensation that covered him. He could still feel the stings, but then they gradually started to fade off.

"I am glad you have come to your senses. You may stand." He raised his hand up like a conductor and Erik rose to his feet like a puppet.

"Why have you been chasing me since I got here? What do you want from me!?" he panted. He leaned on a tree and wiped his lips.

"Well, it seems I am to understand that the reason you cheated me was to return and find your killer."

"Yeah, so?"

"Well, believe it or not, your killer has been apprehended. He is currently at the jailhouse on Falkenburg."

"Wait a minute, they, they got him?"

"Yes, Quince."

Erik slapped his fist into his hand.

"*Yes!* I'm there!"

"*No!*" the being billowed.

Erik turned to him.

"Ha! Victor, you're going to have to kill me to stop me from going over there."

"Ha, as you have so boldly and factually stated earlier, you – my friend - are already dead. But if you insist on remaining cocky about it, then maybe I should take you now."

"No, wait… look, please. I *have* to do this. You don't understand."

The being turned his back to Erik and tried to hide a smirk.

"I cannot allow this," he uttered in a truly Grinch type smile, "… *welllll*, maybe unless we come to some sort of agreement." His voice was deep and Erik could almost hear the grin in his comment.

"Agreement? What are you talking about?"

Erik looked at the ring again, the red light was starting to dim. The being slowly turned back to face Erik, and he had his complete attention now.

"Yes, I take you to him. And you hand him to me." he almost said it in a singing type of way.

"Hand him? What do you mean *hand* him to you?"

The being shined an eerie smile displaying its rotted fangs. Worms were crawling between his teeth and he played with them with his snake-like tongue.

"Dude, to hand him to you, I'd have to, I'd have to kill…"

The being's smile grew the second the word 'kill' exited Erik's mouth. He could see it through the cloaked hood.

"Are you outta your mind? You must me outta your mind."

"It was my understanding that you had intended on doing this anyway. After all, he took your life, it is only fitting, is it not?"

"No, my plan was to get him to justice. I mean once he saw me, he'd freak out and probably have a heart attack like that guy from Sanford and Son used to do, but… I can't kill. And besides since they got him I just wanna make sure that he…"

"That he doesn't escape justice? You know that kind of thing happens every day. Shame, isn't it? But I'll tell you what, Quince - I will sweeten the deal," he pointed at the hospital building; "… your friend will live. She may have supernatural skills, but after all – she is not, how would you say - invincible. But she will live… I will give her life in return. All you have to do is agree to my terms."

"Morgan? You'll spare Morgan?"

"As much as I detest the Reconciler, I will spare her life for one that you give me."

"You're Death; don't you call them when you feel like it?"

"It isn't quite that simple. There's an order in which to follow, and how I detest the order."

"And doesn't this break the order?"

The being grimaced then changed view from Erik to the hospital building.

"You ask too many questions, Quince. The offer is on the table, you must choose."

"What happened to the other guy in the robbery, didn't he die?"

"No, alas... he is sitting in the insane asylum. I let him have a glimpse of me and, ha ha... let's just say he lost his sense of reality. Now what do you say? It's a simple arrangement, a life for a life, your friend for the one who killed you, *hmmm?* You have to admit, this is a delicious deal, isn't it?"

Erik stood, thought about it. Sure, he was angry at the guy that killed him and yes he had even wished he *could* kill him, after all – he was a corpse now, it wouldn't be a crime. It's murder when a living person kills another living person. He rewound that in his head a few times.

"It's murder when a living person kills another living person, it's murder when a living person kills another living person. So, I won't be committing murder, right?"

He hadn't realized it but he said the last sentence out loud.

"Of course not." the being smiled.

Erik looked at him, it truly was gruesome to look at, when someone says the phrase 'you look like death warmed over', Erik was staring at the physical description of it.

"You know ever since I came back, I could feel you, your creepiness all over the place. No matter where I go, I always feel like, somebody's watching me. But you want me to kill... why can't you just leave me alone, you monster!? Sure, I'm mad at the guy, but this isn't what I had planned."

The shadow floated closer to him and was still smiling.

"Are you willing to jeopardize the life of your friend? Her parents will forever know it was your fault. Your friends will blame you. Had you not died and stayed dead – she would not be in the hospital."

"No Jerk, *you* put her there."

"Heh heh, Quince my boy, now who's going to believe that? Now, do we have a deal or not? A life for a life."

Erik knew, deep down inside his soul, if he still had a soul, that he wasn't a killer. No, there had to be another way. Maybe it would be better to leave it alone, they caught the guy, he'll serve his time, maybe get the death penalty, maybe spend the rest of his God-forsaken life in prison and think about the crime he committed. Or... worst case scenario, he could get a really good lawyer and walk. That happens every day. But then, on the other hand, if he agreed to this, then Morgan would wake from her coma and her family could have her again. He saw firsthand what his death did to his family; Morgan's family didn't deserve to go through the same ordeal.

He smiled, for just a second, and thought about the first time he met Morgan Rubens in elementary school, in the lunchroom of the second day of school. He let out a burp so loud that everyone heard it, she was sitting at the table behind him and she burst out in laughter and spit milk all over his shirt. They both were taken to the kitchen to clean up and they both were laughing so loud that the lunch lady, Miss Kay started laughing too. And she was normally in a bad mood, the kids used to say that her face was molded into angry.

The smile slowly faded off when he came back to the moment, thought of her now, lying on that hospital bed and imagining what her mother would go through. But then the vision of his murderer walking out of jail a free man wasn't something he enjoyed either. This was a tough one. Erik dropped his head in deep thought, then looked at the ring again. There was a small speck of red left.

"Geez."

He wasn't sure about this, making decisions was always a hard thing for him, even when he was alive.

"I'm sorry – I can't go through with it, Morgan means the world, but I think I'll just..."

He looked up. The being was gone. He turned around, he was alone out there. Looking at the hospital building, he ran to the window and looked in. Morgan's mother was weeping heavily in the waiting room and Maddie was trying to console her.

"Morgan." he whispered.

He stared at Morgan's mom. He'd known her most of his life, she was almost like a second mother to him at times. His eyebrows curled down in an angry frown. He had a choice to make, and he turned, started walking.

CHAPTER 12

The familiar Honda Odyssey parked in the almost empty lot, aside from a couple of cars, a news truck and several police cruisers, the parking lot for the Falkenburg Jail House was practically empty. She turned off the vehicle.

"I don't know what to do. How do we even go in if we go in what do we do?"

"Well, you know if Erik found out about this, then he's going to show, if he isn't already here, Elizabeth."

Brian turned to the back of the van after he said that Kimmy, Christy and Jordan were there. She'd stopped and got Kimmy after a text to Brian.

"I'll call Dad, he's a deputy, he's probably close by, and he leaves his shift soon." Kimmy said.

The friends stepped out of the van.

"What do we do, Elizabeth?"

"I don't know Kimmy, let me think."

They looked over, the news truck was on, they could hear it humming with the lights on and the reporter was standing out there setting up to start her segment.

"Are you ready Nelson?"

"Yeah, we're live in 3, 2, 1..." the camera man pointed at the reporter.

"Thank you Connie, and yes as you said, we are here at the Falkenburg Jail where the alleged killer of the Brandon teen is being held…"

"What do you mean alleged!?" Brian screamed.

The newscaster turned, the viewers on TV saw her glance over behind the camera.

"Excuse me?"

Brian and Jordan walked up to her, their backs were to the camera.

"That guy killed my best friend, where do you get this *alleged* stuff from?!" Jordan said adjusting his arm in the sling.

"Nelson are we still live?" she asked.

He raised his thumb up. She knew she was on to something.

"The guy in there killed my best friend, I was there. We were all there, right guys?"

Elizabeth, Christy, and Kimmy walked into the light, agreeing with Brian.

"We have breaking news here folks, we have the friends of the murdered teen. In fact, I believe some of you were filmed on an earlier segment at the Jimmy John's, right?"

Brian turned to Elizabeth, she shook her head 'no',

"He had a lot of friends, those could have been anyone from our school, Ma'am." He smiled.

"So young man, uh did you actually witness the murder of your friend?"

"Well… uh, no, but we were…"

"Oh so you didn't actually see the gun man brandish his weapon and pull the trigger?"

"Well, n - no Ma'am, but we…"

"Well then it's *alleged* until you have a true witness or until the perpetrator is proven guilty."

"People were in the bank when it happened, we were across the street. They had a camera in the bank, lady! He did it!"

"Jordan, calm down." Elizabeth said.

"We're trying to get inside. I wanna see this jerk!" Brian fumed.

"These teenagers are here for their friend, the Victoria High student that was killed. They are still in mourning, as you can witness. May I ask you a question?" she pointed at Kimmy, "… this student was a friend of yours, right?"

Kimmy nodded.

"How did you feel when you learned your friend had been killed?"

Kimmy turned to her, then turned back to her friends.

"Really lady?" Jordan asked, "… you know I listen to my parents talk about the news, how you people come up with the most stupid questions, just to get a reaction out of the viewers. Now don't you think that was a stupid question?"

"Jordan, chill. Don't disrespect." Elizabeth said.

"Elizabeth, really? Your friend was gunned down in the middle of the street, in front of a bunch of witnesses, how do you feel about that?

Doesn't that sound ridiculous? Lady if I stomped on your foot with all my might, exactly how would that make you feel? If I told you that you need a new make-up artist, because right about now you look like Chucky from the movie *'Child's Play'*... how would that make you feel?"

"Jordan."

"I'm over this lady, Elizabeth. We're here for Q and she's trying to get a sappy news story out of it, that's pathetic."

"The people have a right to know, young man."

"*Really?* Aside from us and you do you see any other people out here?" he cupped his hands to either side of his mouth and yelled out, "... hello? Any people out there feel the right to know about my friend Q? Anybody?! Come on, we've got some scoop tonight! We've got the press here! Anybody? We want to know how you feel about a teenager being gunned down in public! Somebody say something!?"

He turned to the reporter.

"That settles it, I guess the only one really nosey —oops I mean, curious is you, isn't it?" he smirked sarcastically.

"Jordan, I said chill!" Elizabeth screamed.

"Whatever! My friend is dead and we have freaking Muppet News on the scene. I'm over this lady! Bye Miss Piggy."

He walked toward the building. As he got closer, the door opened and a deputy walked out.

"What's going on out here?" he asked.

"Officer, may we have a word?" the newscaster asked.

"No comment, a press conference will be given for the public and media at eight in the morning, come back then." He said. He turned and looked at the kids and recognized Kimmy.

"Hey, aren't you Jeff's daughter?"

"Yes sir, may we come in?"

"Yeah, come in."

As they walked toward the door, they heard footsteps out in the parking lot not far away. The blinding lights from the camera equipment didn't let them see who it was. He stepped up toward the camera from behind and his foot swiped the tripod stand. It crashed to the pavement and burst into pieces that fell all over the place. The plug for the bright light was pulled along with the tripod falling so it went from blinding bright to blinding dark in a split second.

"Who?"

He walked over the crashing debris. The friends instantly recognized the shape of the head that walked toward them.

"My camera equipment!" the cameraman screamed.

Brian turned to the man.

"Yeah, how do you *feel* about that?"

"Erik!" Elizabeth sighed.

He walked by the group, past the newscaster, who's mouth was gaped open, and he went right up to the open door and walked by the deputy who also stood shocked.

"Erik?" Brian ran in behind him.

The newscaster turned to the deputy.

"Oh my God, that's the dead teen! Then it's true! That's the... Nelson! Grab the other camera from the van! Hurry!" she reached in her pocket for her phone and fumbled trying to get it to video mode.

The friends walked in behind him and she tried to walk in, the deputy closed the door.

"Sorry ma'am, no cameras allowed."

She watched the door close in her face, holding up her phone.

"Erik, why are you here? What are you going to do?"

Erik kept walking and didn't answer Christy.

He stepped to a door and tried to turn the knob, it was locked.

"I'm uh, sorry young man, you can't pass this point."

Erik turned to him, the anger on his face wasn't something he could easily hide and he wasn't in the mood to hide it anyway.

"Erik, what are you going to do?"

He looked at Elizabeth, then turned back to the deputy.

"I need to get in here."

"I'm sorry but I can't allow that, you're a minor and you don't have clearance. Uh, is he really the kid that got..?"

Erik turned back to the door, grabbed the knob and turned it in frustration. They heard the click, a crunch, then the snap, then he pulled back his hand and the knob was in it. He turned and dropped it on the floor.

"Hold it young man." The deputy reached for his belt.

"Really? What are you going to do, shoot me? Didn't you hear? I'm already dead, Officer."

"Officer please, he has to see this man. Please?" Elizabeth pleaded.

"If he can rip a knob off a secured door, what's he going to do to this guy's neck?"

"Erik is not a killer!" Brian screamed, "... uh, are you Erik?"

He rolled his eyes and walked into the hallway. The cop followed and his friends were behind him.

He turned the corner and two detention deputies stepped out.

"Whoa!?"

"Don't shoot guys, there are kids here." The deputy barked.

"I'm sorry, you can't pass this point." They told Erik.

"I have to get inside." He said.

The two men walked up to Erik, he reached out and placed his dead cold hands on their shoulders. The chill traveled throughout their system in seconds and they fell to the floor.

"Snappers, Erik, you killed them!" Kimmy screamed.

Jordan knelt down to one of the men, felt for a pulse, "… no they're still breathing."

The deputy rushed up to Erik.

"Son, I cannot let you pass if you are going to harm anyone."

"I just need to see him, it'll be quick." He uttered.

"Erik, I don't like the look in your eyes, what are you planning to do?"

He turned to Jordan, they had never seen him this serious before.

"This is for Morgan." he said.

Another door opened in front of them and a detective was pulling Daniel S. Keith from the interrogation room. The man turned and saw Erik's face, he stopped in shock, Erik delivered an angry determined smile.

"*Your friend lives if you deliver the man to me.*" He heard the voice of the dark entity in his head.

"You? I killed you!" the man said pointing at Erik.

"It's him!" Jordan yelled, "… let me at him!"

184

Jordan rushed by Brian and jumped at the guy. The deputy tried to stop him and he tackled the man to the floor. The man fell back toward a cop, but Jordan slammed into the side door.

"Ow! My arm!" the teen screamed in pain.

The detective quickly pulled Jordan up but he didn't feel when the killer slipped his weapon from his holster, though he was handcuffed, he now had a gun and was holding it up aimed at them all.

"He has a gun!"

The deputy quickly drew his weapon and held out his other hand to stop the kids from moving forward.

"Kids, get in the room there!" he pointed.

The deputy turned and was rewarded with a hard smack across the skull with the gun, he fell to the floor in a painful thud and blood spurt out of his forehead.

"You guys are going to walk me out of here, or I'll make sure none of you walk out alive."

"Lizzy, go into that room, go guys. You don't need to see this."

"Erik no…"

"Go!"

He walked toward the man.

"I'm warning you, you freak!" he screamed holding out the gun.

Elizabeth and the friends ducked into the room and three more deputies scrambled out into the hallway behind Erik.

"Young man, stand down!" one of them ordered.

"You guys are going to do this my way!" Keith barked. He stood about five feet eight, stocky muscular build and had a tattoo on his left hand that looked like a red thunderbolt. The buzzed haircut looked military and his deep piercing blue eyes were almost scary. His hands shook in a mixture of nervousness and rage as he held the gun.

Erik stared into his eyes, then he glanced down at his ring and it was almost a dull red now.

"I killed you."

"I don't know," Erik smiled, "… maybe you missed."

"I won't this time."

He raised his handcuffed hands and pulled the trigger.

BLAM!

Erik flinched, then smiled. The cops behind Erik ran up, threw him to the floor and covered him with the metal bench and opened fire. From inside the room where the friends were it sounded like a standoff gone badly.

"Erik!?" Elizabeth screamed.

She tried to open the door, Brian held her back.

Within seconds, the firing stopped. It was quiet, then they heard multiple footsteps hurrying down the hallway. Brian shoved open the door and they ran out. Daniel S. Keith lay motionless on the floor. One deputy was hurt, holding his arm and a trickle of blood ran over his fingers. Erik was pulling himself up from behind the metal bench and Christy ran up to him, touched a hole in his shirt.

"Erik, you were shot."

"Yeah, it tickled."

He held out his hand, he was staring at the ring, the red light was almost gone.

"Lizzy, take me to Morgan, hurry."

Brian grabbed his friend's arm and they ran down the hallway.

"Hold it, you can not leave, you are all witnesses, we have an investigation to…"

"Let them go!" ordered a voice behind them.

"Dad!" Kimmy ran up to him, "…you got my text!"

"Yes Honey, I only need one of you to stay here, we can fill out everything with one witness."

"I'll stay,' Christy said, "… you guys get him to Morgan!"

They looked at Kimmy's dad for an ok.

"Go on, go. I'm probably going to get in trouble for this, go."

"Let's go guys."

They rushed out the door and the reporter was at her van, she and the cameraman were picking up the pieces and putting them back in a wheeled case. She turned and saw the group, then rushed to them as they hurried in Elizabeth's van.

"I'm going to sue you for my equipment!"

Erik turned to her.

"Really? Maybe you didn't hear, I'm dead, lady."

They got in the van and Jordan stuck his tongue out at her. Elizabeth floored it. Brian sat in the front, Erik and Kimmy sat in the next seat behind and Jordan was in back. Erik stared straight ahead but was fumbling with his wrist.

"Erik, uh… now that he's… uh dead. Does this mean that you have to… you know?"

Erik turned to Kimmy, he offered a soft smile and stroked the side of her face.

"I'm sorry Kimber, but unfortunately… yes."

He pulled off his watch and reached over to the back seat.

"Here you go, dude."

"What? Erik I was kidding man, I don't want your watch."

"I want you to have it."

"No!"

"Jordan, stop being a jerk." Erik exhaled.

"Don't call me a jerk you creep!"

"Brat!"

"Corpse!"

"Rich kid!"

"Zombie!"

Erik turned to him.

"Man, I'm not a zombie. I hate to break it to you dude, I know you love watching all those zombie movies, but I can tell you straight up. I'm dead, I'm walking dead and I have no desire to taste human flesh. Think about it, a zombie is dead, why would he want to eat? And more than that – why eat humans? For their blood? Blood isn't going to help a zombie come back to life, he's already dead. They didn't think that through."

"Geez thanks, you just ruined all my zombie movies for me."

Erik smiled then he threw the watch over the seat, it landed in Jordan's good hand.

"Now wear it and that's final."

Brian rolled his eyes.

"Erik, what's going to happen to you?"

"I don't know Lizzy, that's why I want, I need to see Morgan, like quick."

"Morgan's in a coma, Erik."

"I think she's probably waking up about now, trust me on this one."

"How would you know?"

BREEP BREEP!

Elizabeth's phone went off, Brian grabbed it.

"Text from Maya."

"Read it." Elizabeth said.

"Morgan is fine, Maddie is in the room with her. She's asking to see Erik, she says hurry."

Elizabeth punched it.

CHAPTER 13

The Honda Odyssey swerved into the parking lot at the Brandon Regional Hospital. There were many clinics in the Brandon area but only one major hospital. Elizabeth hadn't driven this crazy in her whole time of being behind the wheel, but this wasn't a normal week for her or any of her friends. The doors swung open, the friends rushed out.

"Come on Erik!"

They got to the door and Brian turned, Erik wasn't there.

"Guys!?"

He doubled back to the van, stopped at the open door.

"Erik?"

Erik sat there, motionless.

"Q?"

The friends all ran back to the van.

"Erik?" Elizabeth touched him, he didn't move.

"No! Erik! Please?!"

She looked at the ring on his finger, there was a speck of dulled red in the gem.

"Get him out of the car, come on!" Jordan barked.

Kimmy ran back to the hospital and grabbed a wheelchair. In minutes, a stone-cold Erik Quince was sitting in the wheelchair and they were rushing him to Morgan's room.

"Erik, we're almost there. Don't die on me man."

"Brian, he's *already dead*!" they all screamed.

They got to room 215 but weren't prepared for what was there. As soon as they turned the corner and entered the room, the first thing they saw was Morgan sitting up on the bed – and she had visitors. They had burst into the room too fast to retreat and right now, retreat would have been the best thing to do. Elizabeth was first to see…

"Oh! Mr. and Mrs. Quince!"

The couple turned and Gail Quince's expression was one they all should have expected, but the scream was most definitely not.

"Auggggggghhhhh!!"

It was an ear-piercing scream that woke up everyone in the room. People down the hall heard it and an orderly ran to the room, the friends quickly covered Erik with the sheet from Morgan's bed.

"Is there a problem?"

Gail fell into her husband David's arms hysterical in tears.

"No, uh no Sir," Jordan quickly stepped up, "… we were uh, we're excited that Morgan is back up out of her coma is all, it was murder on her hair, see? Carry on my good man." He smiled.

"Oh uh, ok..?"

Brian helped him out of the room and closed the door. Then turned to Erik's mom and rushed her and held her hand.

"We're sorry Mrs. Quince, we're sorry – we, we didn't know you were here! We didn't know…"

She yanked the blanket off. Erik was sitting there almost like a statue, with a stone-dead stare that went straight into Morgan's soul. She hopped off the bed and walked to him.

"Morgan, he wanted to come to you… the guy that killed him, is dead."

"Why did you dig my Pito out of the ground!? What kind of sick children are you!?" Gail screamed.

"Ma'am we didn't dig him out of the ground!" Elizabeth said.

Morgan's mother walked over, she wasn't as perplexed as the other adults in the room, after all, she was Morgan's mother – she'd seen worse. Maddie walked up to him, touched his arm, he was cold to the touch.

"Is this really Erik?"

"Yes it's really Erik, Maddie, he wasn't dead… well ok, ok, ok yes he was, he *was* dead, past tense, **was**, right? But you see, then he came back. So, he wasn't dead, well he *was* dead, but not to us because… he was walking and, running and, uh… Geez, tell them Morgan!" Brian screamed.

Morgan turned to her Mom.

"Mom he was wearing the Parting Stone, see?" she pointed at the ring and as she pointed to it, it slipped off his finger and dropped to the floor. The sound of a ring bouncing on the floor usually meant nothing to anyone, but to Morgan and her friends, they knew what it meant. As it made its final bounce and rolled on the floor to a stop, the friends' faces froze in grief. Erik Jason Quince, 'Q' to his closest and dearest friends - was truly gone this time.

"Erik?" Elizabeth uttered in quickly tear-filled eyes.

"He's... he's gone, isn't he?" Jordan sighed looking at Morgan.

Morgan nodded.

"He wanted to say goodbye to his parents but we didn't let him because we knew it would be a bad idea."

Gail was in tears in her husband's arms and completely inconsolable. He sat her on a chair. Morgan's mom and Maddie were closest to the wheelchair.

"I'm afraid I don't understand." David, Erik's dad shrugged.

"See he was given just a little more time, to be with his friends," Morgan's mom sighed, "... David I can explain but I'll have to sit you and Gail down with my husband so you can truly grasp this whole... thing."

Brian bent down and picked up the ring, he looked at it and the top was now a slick black flat glassy stone with the image of a skull on it. He turned and sadly handed it to Erik's father.

"Your son was my best friend, Mr. Quince... he was my best friend." His eyes started to water.

Elizabeth was crying in Kimmy's arms, Gail Quince was beyond consoling. Morgan approached the wheelchair, stretched out her hand.

"No Morgan... please... don't touch him." Jordan said.

"I have to Jordan."

"I know, but... don't."

Elizabeth walked over and took both Brian and Jordan's arms in hers.

"This is his destiny, he has to go... Morgan... go ahead." She sobbed.

Morgan stepped up to her former best friend, stared in his eyes. He had a motionless dead stare back into her.

"Since life began, we have been wanderers," Morgan started, staring in Erik's eyes, "... we are born, we grow, we live, we die. Some of us don't die, they become the undead. The Parting Stone identifies the undead, the Parting Stone is a beacon to let the undead know they are undead, and the beacon will bring them home, because Death won't allow escapees to run for long. The wearer of the Parting Stone is on borrowed time because Death yearns to bring them home. Erik Jason Quince – you may now go home."

She reached out her hand, it seemed almost like slow motion. Everyone in the room, including Gail Quince witnessed this ritual and saw Morgan's pale thin hand slowly reach Erik's tanned arm. She moved until there was no more space between them, and then she touched him.

All in the room saw what happened next, Erik's skin started to quickly bubble, within the fraction of a second of her touching him, then there was a smell, a stench that covered the whole room in a blinking moment. Then Erik's body disintegrated into ashes that fell to the floor. The ashes looked like a mixture of dark sand and black crystals that gleamed. In a matter of seconds the floor surrounding the wheelchair was covered. To Morgan and her mother, this was nothing new, but to everyone else in the room, it blew their minds.

Erik's mother fainted in her husband's arms.

"Whoa." Jordan said, "… Morgan that was kinda tight."

Brian walked up and knelt on the floor, grabbed a handful of ashes in his hand and just stared at them as they sifted through his fingers. The floor was covered with it.

"He's, he's gone this time Elizabeth, Q's really gone."

She knelt on the floor next to him and they held each other in a long hug. The only sound

heard was of Erik's mothers wails of deep
heartened sorrow and pain.

CHAPTER 14

Hillsboro Memorial Cemetery was at its usual today. It was Tuesday afternoon, the friends had agreed to come here after school to pay their last respects, again.

Elizabeth looked elegant in the long black dress, she had worn it to school, she knew of the plans today, it was her idea. Brian was in his band tuxedo with new shiny black shoes and so was Jordan, who was adjusting the watch on his wrist. Kimmy and Christy walked up behind them, as did Guillermo and Peter on the other side. Morgan's car was next to Elizabeth's and Maddie and Maya had come with her, along with Josh, Rebecca, Billie Jean and Nathaniel - other band mates who had heard about yesterday and wanted to see themselves. They all stared at the gravestone.

"He was like the brother I never had," Brian said, holding a saxophone in his hand that had a single rose sticking out of it, "… he was a good friend."

"Yes, he was a pain, but he was a good friend." Jordan smiled.

"I… I still can't believe he's gone, guys."

"Yeah Maddie, but he's resting now, he's in a better place." Morgan assured them.

Elizabeth reached over to Brian, he handed her the saxophone.

"Ok guys, we do this, in remembrance of Erik, so we never forget. Once a month I'm going to come here and put a rose on his grave."

"Me too, till the day I die." Brian said.

She pulled out the rose and handed the sax to Jordan. She walked up and placed it on the gravestone, then Jordan brought the sax over to her, she cupped her hand under the horn. He tipped it and some of the ashes poured out in her hands. After her, everyone else there but Morgan took a handful. Then they surrounded the grave. Morgan stood closer to the headstone.

"Ashes to ashes, dust to dust," she said, "... you are gone Erik, but you will never be forgotten. Each of us can tell a story that brought you closer into our lives. Live well, rest well. I'll say – see you soon because I never can say goodbye."

They one by one poured the ashes on the grave. Jordan held the empty Yamaha sax in his hand and gave it to Morgan.

"Bro, I'm never going to forget you." he smiled, "it seems lately all I'm saying is goodbye."

One by one they all got back to the cars, Elizabeth and Brian were last, left alone standing there at the grave.

"I'm going to miss him, Brian."

"Me to… you're not alone, Lizzy."

"Hey, no one calls me that but Erik." She poked him in the chest when she said that. Then they turned and walked to the van.

"How about Liz?"

She shook her finger in the air.

"Beth?"

"No."

"Betsy?"

"Brian, get in the van."

"How about Elsbeth, you know, like the old days of yore."

"Brian, shut up."

"Man, you never told Erik to shut up."

She turned the van on.

"I told him to shut up many times."

"But he never did shut up," Jordan said.

"Why are you hatin' on him now?" Maddie said.

"Shut up Maddie."

"You shut up."

"No, you shut up!"

"Guys, will you just please shut up?" Elizabeth said driving out to the road.

EPILOGUE

Mariposa's Bakery. Two days later and after school, Elizabeth, Morgan, Brian and Jordan met at their favorite eatery. Brian had a black eye and Jordan was bothering him about it.

"I can't believe you stood up to Johnny like that Brian, he could have killed you."

"Well, you know Jordan, Erik was right, we have to stand up to jerks like that. I'm just glad I didn't get expelled."

"Yeah but dude, you punched him so hard he fell back into Mrs. Diriscall's rose bushes, after she got them all replaced and looking great again since the last time. Dude, she was pissed!"

"Ha… I know. But she later patted me on the back and congratulated me for bopping him one."

"I'm not even hungry guys." Morgan said, "… I think I'll just get a drink."

"So, are we the new *Quatro,* with Morgan in the fold?" Jordan asked, "… though to be honest, Kimmy and Christy and Peter kinda wanted to be in the group, I was thinking of changing our name to something like.. the Hive."

"The hive?"

"Yeah, we're the Victoria High Wasps and wasps live in a hive."

"I don't know, you guys wanna vote on it?" Elizabeth asked.

"Sure, you in, Brian?"

He didn't answer.

"Brian?" Elizabeth nudged him with her elbow.

"Huh? What?" It was obvious that something or someone outside had his attention.

"We're thinking about voting on whether or not to change our name and if Morgan is…"

"Guys," he interrupted, "… look at that guy over there standing next to the car." He pointed.

"How rude. I was just saying something."

"Elizabeth, I'm serious, look at that guy."

The three friends stared out the window at a man, about twentyish, tall, thick black shoulder length hair and wearing a full suit – standing out in the hot Florida sun.

Jordan turned to Brian.

"So? Ok maybe he looks like Elvis with long hair, but... so?"

"Look at his ring!"

Elizabeth and Jordan's eyes went from the man's face down to his right hand, there was an amber light glowing from the huge ring on his index finger.

"Is that what I think it is?" Elizabeth asked.

"Shoot man, let's go see."

The three friends got up and walked out the door. Seconds later Morgan walked back to the table with a drink in her hand.

"I got Green Tea anybody want... guys? Guys?"

Morgan looked around inside the restaurant, her friend's weren't there, then she turned and glanced out the window. The three friends were actively in conversation with the strange man outside. Morgan noticed and was going to shrug it off thinking maybe he was someone they knew, but then her interest was piqued, and she instantly became glued to the man, she got up, still staring then he raised his hand to push his hair back and the glow of the ring caught her eyes. He turned view from the kids talking to him outside and glanced back at the window and his eyes locked with Morgan's.

"Oh oh," she sighed, "... here we go again."

THE END?

www.ingramcontent.com/pod-product-compliance
Lightning Source LLC
Chambersburg PA
CBHW011501170626
46814CB00008B/2990